Winter's Crimes 20

Winter's Crimes 20

EDITED BY HILARY HALE

A Crime Club Book
DOUBLEDAY
NEW YORK LONDON TORONTO SYDNEY AUCKLAND

A Crime Club Book

PUBLISHED BY DOUBLEDAY

a division of Bantam Doubleday Dell Publishing Group, Inc.

666 Fifth Avenue, New York, New York 10103

DOUBLEDAY and the portrayal of a man with a gun
are trademarks of Doubleday,
a division of Bantam Doubleday Dell Publishing Group, Inc.

Library of Congress Cataloging-in-Publication Data

Winter's crimes 20/edited by Hilary Hale.
    p.   cm.
"A crime club book."
    1. Detective and mystery stories, English.
I. Hale, Hilary. II. Title: Winter's crimes twenty.
PR1309.D4W56   1989   89-32713
823'.087208—dc20   CIP

ISBN 0-385-26211-6

Contents

Editor's Note

Winter's Crimes celebrates its twentieth birthday with stories by the foremost exponents of the contemporary short story.

As always, the stories have been specially commissioned for the anthology, and also as always, the talented authors have produced a sparkling collection of literate mayhem and murder.

It is the combination of the contributors' fertile imaginations and narrative skills which makes my task as editor one of pure pleasure, and I thank them all for creating this entertaining volume.

Hilary Hale

Winter's Crimes 20

An Unmentionable Death

Simon Brett

Harriet Chailey rang the doorbell of number 73 Drefford Road. It was a large Edwardian house in that part of the city where property prices had rocketed in the last decade. Through the open doors of the garage she could see the discreet chromium gleam of a vintage Bentley.

Two undergraduates propped on their bicycles in the street behind her indulged in the common delusion of their age that the whole world wanted to hear what they had to say. They talked loudly of a party that evening, anatomising its probable guest list. The banter was comfortingly familiar. It seemed such a short time ago that she had been in the town to visit Dickie, Dickie before he took his degree, before he started his research. Dickie had talked just like that in those days, in the days before he became obsessed by his subject, in the days when there had been room in his life for something other than work.

But that had been more than five years ago. And now, as she had had to remind herself so many times in the last three days, Dickie was dead.

She felt again the surge of guilt. She should have kept more closely in touch with her younger brother after their parents died. But it had become decreasingly easy to do so. Of latter years it had been almost impossible to get Dickie talking about anything outside his subject. That subject—some detail of Old French syntax—was so obscure that people incautious enough to enquire about it condemned themselves to a half-hour lecture.

Mind you, Dickie had been good at it. A world expert. Invited to conferences all over the globe—Tokyo, San Francisco, even Paris—to give lectures about the subject. Apparently highly respected in academic circles. But, for the average member of the public—that is, for anyone with interests outside that particular crux of Old French syntax—there were no two ways about it, Dickie's obsession had turned him into a bore.

Though maybe, Harriet thought wryly, he wasn't alone in that. A family failing . . . ? She knew she was equally single-minded about her own work at the British Embassy in Rome. Get her on to her special subject and perhaps the effect wasn't so very different . . .

If only they had both relaxed sometimes. Let up for a while. Thought about other things. Taken time to bridge their eight-year age difference, time to get to know each other.

It was too late now for such hopes.

The door of 73 Drefford Road opened to reveal a man in his fifties. He was tweed-suited and round-faced, with white hair worn almost rakishly long. He looked at her quizzically, unsurprised by a visit from a stranger but with no idea as to who she might be.

"Good afternoon. I'm Harriet Chailey," she announced in her startlingly deep, almost masculine voice.

His face instantly composed itself into an expression of compassion.

"I'm so dreadfully sorry about what happened. Do come in." He ushered her across a tall hallway, heavy with dark wood, into a sitting room of subsided leather chairs and piles of overspilling files, rather like the staff room of a prep school. Naive paintings of South American origin hung on the walls, between framed photographs of vintage Bentley rallies.

"My name's Michael Brewer. I was Richard's . . . well, landlord I suppose I have to say, but I hope his friend, too. Do sit down."

"Thank you."

"Could I get you a cup of tea? Or coffee if you'd rather . . . ?"

"No, thank you. I've only just finished lunch."

"Ah." He perched diffidently on the arm of a sofa. "I don't know if Richard ever mentioned me to you in his letters or . . ."

"No. No, we didn't correspond that much, I'm afraid. Rather lost touch over the last few years."

"Yes. Well, of course. Otherwise I'd have known you were his next-of-kin and wouldn't have dreamed of making the arrangements so quickly or . . ."

He petered out, embarrassed, and then, although Harriet had made no accusation, returned to his own defence.

"I feel dreadful. It's just that he'd never mentioned having any family while he was living here. No one in college seemed to know much about his background. He kept himself to himself."

"Yes."

"And since very few people came to visit him here—and those who did were . . . well, didn't seem to be close friends . . . To put it bluntly, it seemed as though I was the nearest to a friend he had, so when it came to funeral arrangements, I thought the quicker everything was sorted out, the better."

Harriet nodded firmly. "I am very grateful to you."

"Take my word for it, please, Miss Chailey, that, had I had any idea that Richard had a sister, I wouldn't have—"

"Of course not. Don't worry. It's just unfortunate. One of those things."

"Yes."

But Michael Brewer didn't look fully comforted. His expression remained anxious, and Harriet felt she should try to put him at his ease. After all, the man had done more than many would have done in the circumstances.

"I really *am* very grateful to you, Mr. Brewer. At least somebody saw to it that my brother had a proper funeral."

"Yes." He shrugged. "Well, it was the least I could do."

"Hm. Was it in the college chapel?"

"The funeral?"

"Yes."

Michael Brewer looked embarrassed. "No. No."

"Oh." Some instinct restrained Harriet from pursuing this. "I would like to see Dickie's—Richard's—grave, Mr. Brewer. You know . . . I mean, pay my last respects, as it were . . ."

His embarrassment grew. "I'm sorry. Your brother's funeral was at a crematorium and . . ."

"Ah." Somehow this was the greatest shock. When the news had come through to the embassy three days before, she had been knocked sideways, but she had clung on to the image of Dickie's body, the thought that even though he was dead, there was something of him left. But now she knew even that perverse comfort to be illusory.

Firmly, remembering her diplomatic training, she shifted the conversation away from this emotive area. "Are you connected with the university yourself, Mr. Brewer?"

"I used to teach a certain amount," he acknowledged. "But, as you have probably read in the press, there have been a lot of cutbacks in education recently. I'm afraid three years ago I was found to be 'surplus to requirements.' "

"Oh, I'm sorry," she said formally. "What was your subject?"

"Spanish."

Harriet gestured to the walls. "Hence the paintings?"

"Yes. I still go to South America most summers."

"Really? I was posted to Bogotá for a while some years back."

"Ah?"

"I'm in the Foreign Office," she explained.

He nodded. "I don't know Bogotá well. Only ever spent a few days there."

"Oh."

The small talk was slowing to a standstill. There was no point in further evasion. "Mr. Brewer," asked Harriet with characteristic directness, "how did my brother die?"

"Erm . . ."

"I mean, what did he die of?"

The man's embarrassment was now painful to witness. "I think," he said eventually, "it said pneumonia on the death certificate. But you'd have to ask his doctor if you want the full details."

Dr. Hart, like his surgery, was a bit run-down and seedy. He and his sports jacket looked tired, as if they had both seen enough of sick-beds and symptoms. He had a full waiting room of coughers and complainers and students with psychosomatic essay crises. The way he kept glancing at his watch left Harriet in no doubt that she had been squeezed in on sufferance.

"Your brother first came to see me about three months ago, I suppose. Complaining of gastric trouble. Diarrhoea, occasional vomiting, he said. I prescribed for him, but he didn't seem to get better. Came in a couple more times, still no improvement. Towards the end, I went and saw him at the house. But by then the pneumonia had set in and . . ."

The doctor shrugged. Another case ended as all cases will eventually end. The only difference was with this one the end had come a little earlier than might have been expected.

"But surely he should have gone into hospital?" Harriet protested.

Dr. Hart nodded wearily. "I tried to persuade him to go in when he came to the surgery. I wanted some tests done. But he didn't want to know about it. Said he hadn't got the time . . ."

"Had to get on with his work . . ."

"Yes. That was it. And by the last time I saw him, I'm afraid he was beyond tests." The doctor sighed. "I'm sorry, Miss Chailey, but if a patient's determined *not* to look after himself, there's not a lot we doctors can do about it."

"No. And there wasn't a post-mortem?"

"There was no need. I had seen your brother just before he died. It wasn't a case of a sudden, unexplained illness."

"No." Harriet was silent for a moment. "Dr. Hart, what do you think made him ill?"

The reply was brusque almost to the point of rudeness. "Self-neglect. As I said, he didn't look after himself. God knows what he ate or when he ate it. I think Mr. Brewer tried to make him eat the occasional proper meal, but most of the time . . . He just let himself go, I'm afraid. And under those circumstances, he would be prey to any infection that came along. He had so weakened himself by the end that the slightest chill could have turned to pneumonia. Your brother led a rather eccentric life, Miss Chailey." Another, undisguised look at the watch. "And now, if you'll excuse me . . ."

Harriet rose from her chair. At the door she stopped.

"You are telling me everything you know, Dr. Hart, aren't you?"

"Yes," he replied gruffly, turning his attention to the pile of notes on his desk. "Of course I am."

"It just seems so sad," Harriet said, pausing in her removal of books from shelves and looking across the chaos of paper covering her late brother's room, "that Dickie never got married. I'm sure if he'd had someone else to think about, he wouldn't have got so immersed in his work. I mean, no wife would have let him get *that* immersed, would she?"

"No," Michael Brewer concurred gently.

"You didn't see any evidence of girl-friends? I mean, no one came round on a regular basis . . . ?"

"Very few people on any sort of basis."

"No. It seems as if my brother was completely sexless."

Michael Brewer grunted agreement.

Harriet sighed. "I know there are people like that. But as a child he was always lively . . . sociable. He must have been dreadfully lonely."

"I honestly don't think he was," said Michael Brewer, offering what comfort he could. "I think his work so absorbed him that he didn't really notice whether he was with people or on his own."

"Hm. It's strange. Somehow, now, the work itself just seems irrelevant." She picked another book off the shelf. "I mean, I can't even understand the titles of these . . . God knows what I'd make of the contents. No doubt they're worth quite a lot, but certainly not to the average man in the street."

"No."

"Do you think there'd be any chance of getting rid of them

through the university? I mean, one of the libraries . . . some-one working in the same field . . . ?"

"I'm sure that'd be possible. Would you like me to handle it, Miss Chailey?"

"Well, if you wouldn't mind, I'd be extremely grateful."

"No problem. Would you be hoping to make some money from the sale?"

"Oh, goodness, no. Just so long as they go somewhere where they're appreciated."

"Of course."

She looked round the room with a kind of hopelessness. "He didn't really have much, did he? I mean, all these files and books and journals, yes, but not much personal stuff."

"No. Obviously there are his clothes and . . . Do you want to check through all those?"

"No, no. I'll give them to Oxfam or . . ."

"Would you like me to organise that, too?"

"Well, it does seem rather an imposition . . ."

"Not at all. I'm on the spot. It's quite easy for me. And you said you had to get back to Rome . . ."

"Yes, I told them it would only be a few days. Compassionate leave."

The thought of all the work piling up in her office came to her with sudden urgency. And the ambassador was giving that party on Saturday. There's no way they'd get it all organised properly without her. Hm, there was a good flight the following after-noon . . .

"Look, you leave it all with me," Michael Brewer said sooth-ingly. "If you're sure there's nothing you want . . ."

"Well, I'd better keep looking. There might be some odd fam-ily photographs or . . ."

"Stay as long as you like. It's no problem."

"Thanks."

Harriet yawned and sneaked a look at her watch. Nearly eight o'clock. Been a long couple of days. Still, she should really keep checking through. There might be something, some memory to keep open the book of her brother's life.

But the thought of the next afternoon's flight had lodged in her mind. Just another half-hour here, she thought with a hint of guilt, and then back to the hotel. Quick dinner, early night, and train to London in the morning. There was nothing for her here.

"Mr. Brewer," she asked diffidently, "about Dickie's illness . . ."

The man stiffened. "Yes . . . ?"

"How long was he actually bedridden at the end?"

"I suppose about three weeks."

"And was he eating properly then?"

"Well, I tried to make him, but he wasn't interested. And when he did eat something, he had difficulty keeping it down."

"It was very good of you to look after him."

Michael Brewer shrugged. "Only sorry I wasn't more effective."

"And he kept on working?"

"Yes. Right to the end. I tried to persuade him to stop, to go into hospital, but . . . he was very strong-willed."

"Yes."

The doorbell rang. With a muttered "Excuse me," Michael Brewer went downstairs. He left the door open, and Harriet could hear the conversation from the hall.

First, Michael Brewer's urbane "Good evening."

Then an unexpected voice. Young, rough, slightly furtive.

"Oh, hello. I was given this address by a friend."

"Really?"

"Friend called Rod."

"Oh?" Apparently the name meant nothing to Michael Brewer.

"He said this was the place to come to . . . Said there was someone here who—"

"I'm sorry. You've been misinformed. I think you have the wrong address. There's no one here who can help you."

Intrigued by the conversation, Harriet had been drawn to the doorway of Dickie's room. Through the banisters she could see the visitor at the front door. A boy in his late teens, spiked black punk hair, torn denim jeans and jacket. A haunted face, an air of twitchiness but, as well, a kind of insolence.

As she looked, Michael Brewer closed the front door. Harriet went back hastily into the room and, to look busy, knelt down by a pile of files at the foot of a bookcase. She tugged to dislodge them and released a pile of glossy magazines from under the files.

She opened one.

In spite of her occasionally spinsterish manner, Harriet Chailey's experience of life had been broader than might be supposed. She recognised pornography when she saw it.

But she had never seen pornography like this before. There were no female bodies in the pictures. They were all men.

She reached further under the bookcase and pulled out a thin cigar box. Lifting the lid revealed a couple of plastic syringes, some blood-stained bandages, and a small polythene bag with dregs of white powder at the bottom.

"Ah."

She turned to see Michael Brewer framed in the doorway. His face was a mask of pity.

"I'm sorry," he said. "I thought I'd got rid of all that stuff. I was hoping you wouldn't have to find out about it."

"What?" asked Harriet, bewildered. "Do you mean that Dickie died from a drug overdose?"

"No," Michael Brewer replied sadly. "No. That wasn't it."

"I still find it hard to believe," said Harriet. "I mean, from what I remember of Dickie . . ."

"You said you hadn't seen him for a long time . . ." Michael Brewer's voice was gentle and compassionate.

"True."

"And you said it seemed odd that there was no sexual dimension to his life . . ."

"Yes . . ."

"No, I'm sorry. From the time he moved in, there was no question about it."

"Oh."

"Boys used to call here. Ask any of the neighbours. Young men calling late at night. For your brother."

"I see." A thought struck her. "You mean . . . was that young man this evening . . . ?"

Michael Brewer nodded. "I'm sorry. I really didn't want you to find out about it."

"Better I should know."

"Why? Why do you say that? I'd have thought you'd got enough to come to terms with . . . just having heard your brother's died . . . without *this*."

"No. I want to find out as much as I can about him. I regret I didn't get to know him better while he was alive. Now I just want to find out everything about Dickie."

"Ah."

"Maybe it's my way of coping with the bereavement."

"Maybe . . ." Michael Brewer shook his head sorrowfully. "I think you may just be making more pain for yourself."

"Perhaps I need the pain. As a kind of expiation. Punishment for not having got to know him while he was alive."

Michael Brewer nodded, accepting this interpretation.

"Why didn't Dr. Hart tell me?"

"We discussed it, Miss Chailey. We both felt the less people who knew, the better."

"That was not very professional of him, as a doctor."

"Perhaps not. But as a human being . . . well, it was at least compassionate."

"Yes." Harriet looked at her watch. "He wouldn't still be at the surgery, would he?"

"No."

"Do you have his home phone number?"

"Yes," said Michael Brewer, with a rueful nod.

"Are you saying you didn't make the diagnosis straight away?"

"All right, I am, yes." Dr. Hart's voice was testy. He was annoyed enough at being rung at home; and now to have his professional expertise questioned was even more annoying. "Look, Miss Chailey, have you any idea how many patients I see in a day? I get them all through—pensioners with arthritis, menopausal women, students with God knows what problems. Sex, depression, drugs—have you any idea of the scale of the drugs problem in this university? And it just gets worse and worse, because the pushers never seem to get caught—or as soon as one is caught, another two appear to take his place.

"Well, as a result of all this, there's not a lot of time, you know. So, on the whole, as a doctor, you go for the obvious. Someone comes in complaining of diarrhoea, you tend to prescribe something for diarrhoea. Look, for God's sake, until just before he died, I didn't even know your brother was homosexual."

"Nor did I."

"No. Well, there you are. You grew up with him and didn't know. I met him for what . . . three . . . four ten-minute consultations? So how am I expected to know every detail of his life?"

"I see your point—I mean the drugs thing . . . That's the biggest shock to me. He used to be so anti-drugs. Really priggish about it. Still, I suppose I'm talking about a long time ago."

"People change."

"Yes. Did you know about his drug habit?"

"Again, not till the end, no. If I had known, I might have been able to do something about it."

"Did Michael Brewer tell you?"

"No. God, he tried to keep it from me. He did everything to try and stop me from finding out."

"Why?"

"Because he was a good friend to your brother."

"He wasn't more than that, was he?"

"What do you mean?"

Michael Brewer had left Harriet discreetly alone in his study to make the phone call, so she felt she could risk this line of questioning. "Well," she continued, "we've established that Dickie was gay . . ."

"No. Absolutely not. I'm certain Michael isn't. No, he's just that rarity in this day and age—a good man. He found himself in the situation of having a sick man on his hands, and he just did his best to look after that sick man."

"But if Michael didn't tell you, how did you find out about the drugs?"

"I . . . came across some stuff in your brother's room. Syringes, what have you . . ." Just as I did, thought Harriet, as the doctor went on, "Michael Brewer wasn't even there at the time."

"Did you talk to Dickie about it?"

"No. He was too far gone with the pneumonia by then. Virtually unconscious."

"But surely that was the time to get him into hospital?"

"Look, Miss Chailey, your brother was going to die. There was nothing I could do about it, nothing anyone could do about it at that stage. I agreed with Michael Brewer that it would be more compassionate to let him die in his own surroundings than in the exposed anonymity of a hospital ward."

"And was another consideration the fact that you didn't want your failure to be known to the hospital doctors?"

"Failure? What do you mean, Miss Chailey?"

"I mean your failure to diagnose earlier what was really wrong with Dickie."

There was a silence from the other end of the line. Then, grudgingly, Dr. Hart conceded, "All right. Yes. I should have been alert to it, and I wasn't. As I say, so many people come through the surgery. With some types you're immediately suspicious. You spot them as high-risk the minute they walk in. But with someone like your brother . . . who seemed so . . . well, eccentric, yes, but otherwise quite ordinary . . . I mean, the last person you would associate with either homosexuality or drugs."

"True," Harriet agreed. "And it was because you didn't want your mistake shown up that you signed the death certificate with pneumonia and—"

"Pneumonia was what he died of," Dr. Hart objected.

"All right, that was what he died of, but it wasn't what killed him."

"You're splitting hairs."

"No, I'm not." Harriet pressed on relentlessly. "And for the same reason you were happy to see the funeral arrangements made as quickly as possible? Happy that he should be cremated? To destroy the evidence of your blunder?"

"All right. If that's how you choose to put it, yes."

There was a silence after this admission. Then the doctor came again to his own defence. "Listen, Miss Chailey, I don't feel particularly proud of how I've behaved over this. But AIDS is a new disease, it's currently an incurable disease, about which your average GP—and I've never claimed to be more than your average GP—knows very little. Now, if a known drug addict—or one of the local rent boys—comes into my surgery complaining of diarrhoea or weight loss . . . all right, I'm on my guard. With someone like your brother," he repeated, "when he comes in with something that could be caused by food poisoning or one of any number of viruses, well . . ."

"Yes." Harriet sighed. Through her anger and frustration, she couldn't help seeing the doctor's point of view. "And how do you suppose my brother contracted it?" she asked dully.

"Take your pick. Given his promiscuous, active homosexuality . . . given the fact that he'd been to a conference in San Francisco within the last year . . . given the drug habit . . . given all the facts I didn't know about him until just before he died . . . he was a prime target."

"Yes." Harriet felt empty and listless. "Well, thank you, Doctor, for telling me the truth."

"I'm sorry I didn't tell you first time round, but . . . quite honestly, I really didn't think it was necessary for you to know something that could only cause you pain."

"Thanks for the thought."

The doctor cleared his throat at the other end of the line. "If it's any comfort to you, Miss Chailey," he said, "you've made me feel an incompetent old fool."

Harriet wasn't hungry when she got back to her hotel that night. The quick dinner she had been promising herself had lost its appeal. So had the early night. The revelations of the evening had made sleep a very distant possibility.

Even the next day's flight to Rome had become remote and unimportant. The ambassador's party on Saturday had lost its urgency. It would still happen somehow, whether she was there or not.

The fact that her brother had died of AIDS made everything else seem trivial.

She had found almost nothing of personal relevance in his room. Just his keys. Still, she noticed with a pang as she put them in her handbag that they were attached to the brass Italian key-ring she had given him for a birthday in the days when they still remembered each other's birthdays.

Ironically, the only other items she had brought from 73 Drefford Road were the gay magazines and the box of drug equipment. In a perverse way, as if it made any difference at this stage of her brother's life (or rather death), she felt she should remove this incriminating evidence from his room.

She glanced through the magazines, not disgusted or intrigued by their contents, just bewildered. And bewildered at the sidelights they offered on her brother's life. How little she had known him.

The magazines, she noticed, went in sequence. Published every month. Dickie's collection covered the last six months. Maybe there had once been other back numbers. Michael Brewer had implied that he had checked through the room to remove all the evidence of homosexuality he could find. He had presumably only missed this lot because they were jammed under the files.

Abstractedly, trying to control and organise her thoughts, Harriet placed the magazines in order. She put down the oldest first. Six months ago, five months, four months, three months, two months. Then the latest.

She looked at the cover of the most recent magazine and felt a sudden dryness in her mouth. Oh my God, she thought

The taxi driver seemed confused by her request.

"It's not that I don't know where to take you," he said. "It's just you don't seem the sort to want to go there."

"I know where I want to go," said Harriet, firmness as ever further deepening her husky voice.

This seemed to explain things for the taxi driver. "Oh," he said to her considerable amusement, "I get it. You're one of them transsexuals, aren't you?"

It was a small pub behind the bus station. Small and run-down. Outside motor bikes clustered like insects round a rotten fruit.

Harriet's determination was so strong that she didn't stop to think how incongruous her smart Italian coat must look amidst the studded leather and frayed denim of the interior. As she ordered a red wine, she was unaware of the quizzical eyebrows of the ear-ringed and heavily moustached barman or of the open amazement and muttered comments of the other drinkers.

She looked eagerly round the bar. There were a few other women, though their livid, streak-dyed hair and black vampire make-up gave them the look of another species from her own. But most of the occupants of the bar were male. Young men with blonded hair and haggard eyes, shrieking jokey insults at each other. Thickset men in heavy leathers. Older men in furtive raincoats.

She tried to imagine Dickie in this environment. She tried to picture the young man she remembered from her childhood leaning twitchily against the bar like these other men, but her mind could not encompass the image.

And then she saw it.

A familiar, haunted face. Pained and putty-coloured under black spiked hair. The boy sat alone, uninterested in the half of beer in his hand. His eyes darted anxiously around the bar.

Harriet Chailey moved across to sit beside him. He gave no sign of having noticed her.

She touched his arm. He recoiled as if she'd burnt him, and the sunken, paranoid eyes found hers.

"What do you want?" he hissed.

"I want to talk to you."

"I haven't done nothing wrong. I haven't got nothing on me."

Their dialogue was attracting attention from the drinkers around them, who seemed to bristle and move almost imperceptibly closer. The atmosphere was not friendly.

"I just want to talk," Harriet persisted, again placing a gentle hand on the boy's denim sleeve.

This time he sprang to his feet, and a flicker of menace went through the watching crowd.

"I'll pay you," said Harriet.

The hollow eyes turned back to her.

"Money?"

She nodded.

"How much?"

"Twenty pounds."

The boy nodded and sat back down again. As he did so, he flicked a message with his head to the protective crowd around him. They relaxed and returned to their drinks.

"What do you want to know?" he asked truculently.

"I want to know about 73 Drefford Road," said Harriet.

Michael Brewer came back from the shops the next morning and let himself in through the front door of 73 Drefford Road. As he closed it, he was shocked to hear a deep female voice from the top of the stairs.

"Good morning."

He spun round to face her. "Miss Chailey."

"I apologise for letting myself in. I had Dickie's keys."

"Of course. I must confess to being somewhat surprised to see you. I understood that you were catching a plane back to Rome this afternoon."

"That was my intention, yes."

"And can I ask what made you change your mind?"

"If you come up to Dickie's room, I'll tell you."

"Very well." Michael Brewer nodded slowly. "Will you just allow me to put my shopping in the kitchen?"

"Of course."

"Can I offer you a cup of coffee or anything of the sort?"

"No, thank you."

Harriet was sitting in an armchair in front of the bathroom door when Michael Brewer entered his late tenant's room. "Now," he asked amiably, apparently unperturbed by her trespass, "what is this? Is there something else of Richard's you want to look for? Or something you've found and want to show me . . . ?"

"This is the only thing I want to show you." She indicated the latest edition of the gay magazine on the table beside her.

"Oh?"

"But time enough for that. Do sit down."

"Thank you," said Michael Brewer, acting on the invitation.

"I'm sorry. It's ridiculous my offering you a chair in your own house."

He shrugged to indicate that he was unworried by this social solecism. "Well, now . . . ?" He raised a quizzical eyebrow.

"I just wanted to say how much care you put into looking after Dickie, and . . ."

He made a gesture of self-depreciation. "The least I could do."

"Yes. How soon did you realise what was actually wrong with him?"

"I didn't have any suspicions until near the end. I should have thought of it earlier. You know, knowing the life he led. I mean, when he started getting recurrent diarrhoea . . ."

"Losing weight . . ."

"Yes. And also getting this sort of skin infection . . . I should have put two and two together . . . But I'm afraid I didn't. Until it was too late."

"Do you think Dickie himself knew what was wrong with him?"

"No, I'm sure he had no idea. Right up to the end. I certainly didn't say anything about it to him. I wanted to spare him as much pain as I could."

"That was very thoughtful."

"Well . . . Anyway, Richard didn't really think about his health. For him being ill was just an inconvenience . . ."

"Something that kept him from the dissection of Old French syntax?"

"Precisely."

"It was unfortunate, Mr. Brewer, that Dr. Hart didn't spot what was really wrong with Dickie."

"Yes. Perhaps it was."

"Didn't you feel that you should share your suspicions with him the minute you realised what it was?"

"I did think about that, yes. But, quite honestly—and this may have been very wrong of me—by the time I realised what was happening, which was very near the end, I thought it better to keep quiet. I mean, the point is, with AIDS, there is no cure. Richard was under a death sentence from the moment he contracted the dreadful thing. And, given a choice between having a load of tests, being labelled as a plague victim, being hospitalised —and the alternative, which was dying with a degree of dignity . . ."

"And in ignorance . . ."

"Yes. Well, I'm afraid I chose the second course."

"Hm." Harriet looked pensive. "It's a strange disease, AIDS. Nobody yet knows much about it."

"No. That's what makes it so terrifying."

"Yes. There have even been cases of pathologists refusing to do post-mortems on AIDS victims."

"So I've heard."

"And I dare say ordinary doctors aren't immune from that kind of fear. They're only human, after all. I dare say some of them would rather not investigate an AIDS patient too closely."

"Maybe not."

"And be quite happy if the victim's body is disposed of as soon as possible without too many questions asked."

"I suppose that could happen, yes."

"The other strange thing is that a lot of the symptoms—at least the early symptoms—could be mistaken for all kinds of other ailments."

"So I believe."

"Did you know, for instance," said Harriet suddenly, "that systematic poisoning could produce a lot of the same symptoms as AIDS?"

There was a half-beat pause before Michael Brewer replied, "No. No, I didn't."

"Arsenic, for instance."

"Really?"

"Oh yes. Diarrhoea . . . vomiting . . . weight-loss certainly, because the victim can't keep anything down . . . discoloration of the skin . . . dermatitis—all classic symptoms of arsenic poisoning. So long as the case wasn't investigated too closely, it would be quite easy to confuse the symptoms."

"Oh." Michael Brewer smiled urbanely. "What a mine of information you are, Miss Chailey. I'm sure you're very good at Trivial Pursuit."

"Thank you. Yes, I'm not bad at it."

"But, of course, I believe that nowadays it is extremely difficult to obtain arsenic in this country, so I can't imagine that the confusion you describe would be very likely ever to occur in real life."

"No. No. Mind you, in other countries arsenic is still relatively easy to obtain."

"Really? Another Trivial Pursuit answer?"

"No. All I'm saying is that smuggling arsenic into this country would be quite as easy as—perhaps even easier than—smuggling in other illegal substances."

Michael Brewer was icily silent. When he finally spoke, there was a new, cold detachment in his voice. "May I ask precisely what you're saying, Miss Chailey?"

"What I'm saying is that there is a lot of drug abuse in this city. In the university and with the local youngsters."

"So I've heard."

"And the young people must get their supplies from somewhere . . ."

"Presumably."

"One of their sources is this address—73 Drefford Road."

"What?" His face was suddenly pale. "Where did you hear that from?"

"A young addict."

"You can't believe what they say!"

"I believed this one. He was the boy who came round here last night."

"He wasn't looking for drugs. He was—"

Harriet overruled him. "The boy was looking for drugs. He told me. Oh, you played it very cleverly, yes. You made it seem as if he was a rent boy coming round looking for Dickie. But he wasn't. He was after drugs. Just like all the other late-night visitors to this house."

"But your brother—"

"My brother wasn't homosexual."

"Look, I know it's hard for you to believe that a member of your family—"

"You can stop all that, Mr. Brewer. There's no point in trying to maintain that pretence any longer. I know what's been going on here."

"Oh?" The voice was icier than ever.

"You've been smuggling in drugs from South America for some years. I don't know how long, but certainly since you lost your job."

"What do you mean?"

"Come on, Mr. Brewer. Vintage Bentleys are an expensive hobby. You need a fairly healthy income from somewhere to keep that going."

"But I—"

"Good little system you had worked out. All ticking over fine. Until Dickie found out what you were up to. He'd always hated drugs, hated what they did to people, and I think he must have threatened to expose what you were doing."

"You don't know what you're talking about."

"Yes I do," said Harriet implacably. "You fobbed Dickie off for a while . . . maybe said you'd stop dealing, maybe said you'd confess voluntarily . . . somehow you bought time. But my brother remained a threat . . . until you saw a way of getting rid of him—a way which would never be investigated too closely. You started systematically to poison him and at the same time worked out how to make it appear that he was in a high-risk category for catching AIDS."

Michael Brewer was calmer now. Once again he had control of himself. He rubbed his chin reflectively. "Say that what you're suggesting was true . . . what was it that started you thinking that way?"

"Two things," Harriet replied firmly. "First"—she pointed at it—"this magazine."

"What about it?"

"Good idea, getting the magazines. I think you built up the collection privately, then slipped them into this room towards the end, when Dickie was too ill to notice what was going on. You hid them, but you didn't hide them too well. Hid them just badly enough, in fact, so that Dr. Hart couldn't fail to find them. Just as I couldn't fail to find them yesterday."

"You have no proof of that."

"But I think I do. Circumstantial evidence, at least."

"Oh?"

"You see, this one"—again she indicated the magazine on the table—"was only published a fortnight ago . . ."

"But—"

"And by then Dickie was far too ill to get out of bed—let alone go out and buy magazines."

"Ah." Michael Brewer nodded ruefully, acknowledging his carelessness. "You mentioned two things . . ." He was now almost diffident in his casualness.

"The other thing was the drugs."

"Oh?"

"That made me suspicious. It seemed like overkill. All right, we all know by now—no one could help knowing from all the publicity campaigns—that AIDS can be contracted by promiscuous homosexual activity or by drug addicts sharing needles. One or other would have been good enough to start people wondering about the nature of Dickie's illness. To build him up as both a promiscuous gay *and* an intravenous drug abuser seemed excessive. It also started me thinking that perhaps you had access to drugs yourself."

"Ah!" Michael Brewer bowed his head contritely. "Yes, I agree that was maybe a bit over the top."

"You realise," said Harriet, "that what you've just said is tantamount to an admission that you did kill my brother?"

"Yes." He smiled grimly. "Yes, I realise that." Slowly, he started to loosen his tie. "And you must realise why I am not afraid to make that admission to you."

"The admission that you killed Dickie?"

"Yes. I killed him. And I can tell you that in complete confidence, because, I'm afraid, Miss Chailey, there is no chance that you are going to leave this house alive."

He tugged savagely at one end of his tie, which came loose and flicked out across the room like a whip.

"You're going to kill me too?"

"You've left me no alternative. Just as your brother left me no alternative. I had to kill him, I'm afraid. Self-protection. It's dog-eat-dog out there, you know."

"I know," said Harriet. "I do work for the British Foreign Office, after all."

Michael Brewer smiled condescendingly as he started to wind the ends of the tie around his hands. "Always worth trying a little joke, isn't it? Playing for time. Won't work, but worth trying."

"Strangling," observed Harriet, "won't be nearly such a good murder as the other one. Not nearly so ingenious. And all that dreadful business of getting rid of the body to cope with."

"Needs must when the devil drives, my dear." Michael Brewer moved slowly towards her. "And, though I appreciate your concern, don't worry, I'll think of something."

"What's more," Harriet went on gamely, "I don't think even Dr. Hart will sign a death certificate describing a strangling as 'natural causes.' "

"NO, HE BLOODY WELL WON'T!"

The new voice took them both by surprise, as the bathroom door was flung open and Dr. Hart crashed into the room.

Michael Brewer gazed at the apparition with his mouth open. It closed with a snap as Dr. Hart's fist caught him on the point of the jaw. The murderer crumpled backwards in a heap and offered no resistance as the doctor plunged a syringe into his wrist.

"That'll keep him quiet till the police come."

"Good heavens," said Harriet.

Dr. Hart looked slightly sheepish. "I'm sorry. I'm not normally a violent man, but I'm afraid, with drugs, I just see red. When I hit him I was hitting all the pushers in the world. When I think of the wreckage of young lives which I've seen pass through my surgery . . ."

"Yes. Are you sure it was all recorded?"

"Certain." He went back into the bathroom and emerged with a cassette recorder. He spooled it back some way and pressed the Play button. Michael Brewer's confession was reassuringly repeated.

Harriet looked wistfully around the room. "I'll never forgive myself," she said, "for not getting to know Dickie better, but at least now I'll know that what I remember of him was what he was really like."

"Yes." Dr. Hart looked at her. "Thank you for asking me to help."

"There was no one else I could ask."

"No. Still, at least I feel I've done something. I told you how you made me feel last night . . ."

"Yes."

"Well, at least this morning I feel less of an incompetent old fool." He gave her a weary grin. "Marginally less, anyway."

Justice in My Own Hands

E. X. Ferrars

I have never committed a murder.

I once took justice into my own hands, and if this had happened fifty years ago, it might have led to something which perhaps could be described as murder, since capital punishment then was still normal. And to send a person to the gallows, even if this was deserved according to the law, might have been regarded in its way as homicidal. But a sentence for what is called life, but which is a mere ten years or so, with time off for good behaviour, is altogether a different thing. Only too different, I realise, as the years pass . . .

It is about eight years ago now that my Grandaunt Emma telephoned me one morning and begged me pressingly to come and see her.

"Dorothy, dear, I know you're very busy, but couldn't you spare a couple of days to come down here at the weekend?" she said. "You know I've not been well, don't you, and there's something I want to talk to you about before . . . well, as soon as possible."

Her old voice creaked and was a little shaky. She was eighty-six, and a few months before—as I had heard from my sister Marion, who lived with her—had suffered a slight stroke. Considering her age, the old woman had made a very good recovery. She had apparently become a little more absent-minded than before, but had not been paralysed in any way and could still enjoy reading and watching television, and could even walk around the house a little without assistance.

She had had to give up cooking, which irked her because it had been one of the main interests in her life. At one time she had even written articles about it for one of the women's magazines. And she had stubbornly gone on with it until her stroke, since when, unfortunately for Marion—who could produce a very presentable shepherd's pie and even grill a chop with some success—Aunt Emma had become more critical than ever and not as grateful as she might have been for all that Marion did for her.

If the telephone call that morning had been a cry for help from Marion, badly wanting a few days off to meet some friends, go to a theatre, and do some shopping in London, it would have puzzled me less than our aunt's anxious invitation.

For anxious it certainly was. It sounded almost frightened. The stroke, I thought, must have affected her more than Marion had told me, more perhaps than Marion, spending as much time as she did with the old woman and being too used to her to notice a gradual change, had even realised. Aunt Emma had always been an intrepid character, always busy with half a dozen worthy causes, and had once stood for Parliament as an independent candidate. She had lost her deposit but had always referred to the experience as if it gave her some kind of special importance. Apart from that, she was rich, generous, and affectionate.

"Yes, of course I could come if you really want me," I said, "though it isn't just the easiest thing at the moment."

"Please, Dorothy, please!" she implored. "This weekend. Can't you do it?"

I could if it was really that urgent, though I usually worked over the weekend. At that time I was employed by a literary agent and often took manuscripts home with me on Fridays to read in the quiet of my small flat in Hampstead. In the office there were always interruptions, telephone calls, committee meetings, visiting authors, discussions with publishers. And recently I had been letting the manuscripts pile up . . . But if it was really that important to Aunt Emma, the manuscripts would just have to wait.

"Very well," I said. "On Saturday morning, will that be all right?"

"Yes, yes, if you can't come sooner. Couldn't you come on Friday evening?"

"I suppose I could."

"Then, do! Come in time for dinner. After all, it's only an hour from London and you can take a taxi from the station."

"Can't Charles or Marion meet me with the car? I think there's a train at six which gets to Oxford just after seven."

"Perhaps they could. Yes. No. I don't know. I'll speak to them about it." The anxiety in her voice was almost strident.

"You mean you haven't said anything yet about this visit of mine to Marion?" I said.

"How could I, till I knew you'd come?"

That made sense, but I had a sudden uncomfortable feeling that with her new absent-mindedness Aunt Emma might forget to mention my visit to my sister, which might be inconvenient, if not actually upsetting, for her. So I suggested that if Marion was in at that moment, perhaps I might have a few words with her—but Aunt Emma replied in an odd, hurried way that she was not in, and anyway, there were always lots of taxis at the station. So I accepted it and left it at that. I could telephone Marion later, I thought.

I called her that evening, but it turned out to have been unnecessary. Aunt Emma *had* told her of my plans. I was not sure, though, that Marion sounded too pleased.

"But what's she so worried about?" I asked. "Because she is worried, isn't she?"

"I think it's just that she's got it into her head that she's bound to have another stroke soon," Marion answered, "and she wants to be sure of seeing you once more before it happens. You were always her favourite, you know."

I did know it. Marion, living with her in Oxford, had always done far more for Aunt Emma than I had, yet we both knew that I occupied a place in her affections that Marion could never come close to.

"Well, I'll see you on Friday," I said, "and don't bother about meeting me. I'll take a taxi."

"Oh, I'll meet you," she said, "or else Charles will."

In the event, it was Charles who came to the station.

I had never been able to make up my mind about Charles. There had been a time when I had thought that he was in love with me, but it was Marion whom he had married. However, this had not done much more than damage my *amour propre*, leaving my heart intact. He was an oddly nondescript kind of man, fairly tall, fairly thin, rather stooping, with grey eyes, and a long, pale face topped by shaggy fair hair which always looked as if he had forgotten to have it cut rather than deliberately let it grow long. He was a university lecturer in social history and, according to some people, was brilliant, as would be generally recognised, they said, when he finished his book.

Unfortunately, the book showed no signs of ever nearing an end, and that, to someone in my profession, only too used to people who at some future date were going to produce a work of genius, was no recommendation. All the same, I had always found him a curiously exciting man, though I could not have said why. Perhaps it was his air of wary detachment, his cautious avoidance of becoming more than superficially involved with anyone. It was a kind of challenge.

"It's good of you to come," he said, as we drove away from the station. "The poor old think seems to want you badly. She's made up her mind she hasn't long to live and God knows I hate to say it, but I suppose she's right. When it happens, it's going to be what people call a merciful release. Don't you find that a disgusting phrase?"

"I hadn't realised, from what Marion told me, that she was as ill as that," I said.

"I'm not sure that she is. But she thinks she is, which is what counts. I believe every night when she goes to sleep, she says to herself that she probably won't wake up in the morning. "If I should die before I wake, I beg the Lord my soul to take . . ." I believe death is on her mind all the time, frightening her out of her wits."

But he was wrong. It was not death that was frightening Aunt Emma. It was something which I personally found more horrible. She was afraid of going mad.

I discovered this during the first talk I had alone with her in her bedroom after the dinner that she and Charles and Marion and I had together in the stately but somehow unwelcoming dining room. Charles and I had arrived at the house in North Oxford, in Elwell Street, which is a turning off the Banbury Road, at about a quarter past seven, and we had found Aunt Emma sitting by the fire in the drawing room, dressed in a pretty flowered blouse and a long black skirt, from under the hem of which woolly bedroom slippers protruded. The slippers and the stick which was propped against her chair were the only indications that she was not as well as she had been when I saw her last. She had always been proud of her feet and ankles and would never have appeared in public in anything but the most elegant of shoes, probably Italian and very expensive.

The blouse looked new, however, as if she had been shopping not long before, and her white hair was cleverly cut, while her small, wrinkled face, with its pointed features and dazzlingly blue eyes, showed no signs of recent illness.

Marion joined us briefly, but said that she was busy in the kitchen and soon left us. We had drinks and chatted about my journey, about the recent cold spell, about the shocking cost of nearly everything and the state of the country, and pretended that there was nothing amiss.

Marion and I were rather alike to look at, though I was slightly the taller and two years the older. Actually, I am the same age as Charles, who at that time was forty. She and I were both brown-haired and brown-eyed, with oval faces which no one could call distinguished, long, thin necks, and narrow, sloping shoulders. We were slim and, I suppose, might have made something of this, but neither of us had much dress sense; however, I had learnt to manage a little better than Marion, having found that there was some virtue in it if you worked in a London office, whereas in North Oxford it seemed not to be very important. I had also learnt to cook somewhat better than she had. What she gave us that evening was soup out of a tin, Irish stew, trifle made with custard powder, and instant coffee.

As soon as the meal was over Aunt Emma said that she was sorry but she was very tired and was going straight to bed and hoped that perhaps I would come upstairs presently and talk to her for a little. I helped Marion clear the table and stack the dishwasher, waited for about half an hour, then went up to Aunt Emma's bedroom.

She looked very small and shrunken in the big bed, propped up against several pillows. She wore a pale blue quilted bedjacket and had a book open on her knee, but I noticed that she had not put on her spectacles, so she could not have been reading. They were on the table on the far side of the bed under a lamp which was the only light in the room. As I sat down beside her she closed the book and put it on the table, then reached out and took my hand. Her small, thin fingers dug almost painfully into my wrist.

"Dorothy, do you understand why I wanted to see you?" she asked with a disturbing note of excitement in her usually calm though creaky voice. "My dear, I think I'm going out of my mind."

I gave a laugh, which I dare say sounded rather patronising, patted her hand, and said, "Aunt Emma, you're probably the sanest person I know."

Then I realised that she was serious and wished I had chosen a different tone.

"It's just from time to time," she went on as if I had not spoken. "I don't think the others have noticed it yet. I have these black-outs. Suddenly I can't remember anything. I find myself in the middle of a room and I can't remember how I got there or where I was going. And I begin a sentence and get lost half-way through it and I begin to wonder if it sounds as nonsensical to other people as it does to me. And sometimes it's worse than that. I *see* things . . . Only yesterday I saw poor Bertram standing at the end of the bed, pointing at me and laughing at me. As if he would ever do such a thing! But I knew it was an illusion, I knew it as well as I know you're really sitting here beside me, but I couldn't make him go away." Her voice rose slightly. "Dorothy, I'm so frightened they'll find out and then I'll be helpless!"

Bertram was her long-dead husband. It was from him that she had inherited her wealth. He had died of viral pneumonia about thirty years ago.

"Does it matter if they do find out?" I asked. "They'll take care of you. You aren't frightened they'll try to put you into a mental home or something like that, are you? People can't do that sort of thing nowadays. It's extremely difficult to have a person put into one of those places if they don't want to go, even when they're truly crazy. And you know no one could say that about you. Anyway, Marion and Charles have always been very good to you, haven't they?"

"But there's the money, you see."

I did not see at once, though I recognised that most things in the end come down to money.

She withdrew her hand from mine and crossed it with the other on the hump her knees made in the bed.

"What I want, Dorothy, is to give you power of attorney over my affairs," she said. "Will you see to that for me?"

I was very puzzled.

"Of course," I said, "but wouldn't it be better to give it to Charles and Marion?"

"I don't think you understand," she said. "You can't give power of attorney to anyone unless it's evident that you're in your right mind and you know what you're doing. And I'm afraid if I wait, perhaps . . . perhaps . . . well, I told you, I get frightened sometimes that I'm not quite sane any more and that perhaps I'm going to get worse. You know, I really wish that stroke had finished me off. It would have made everything so much simpler. But if I don't give power of attorney soon to someone, there may be a terrible muddle to clear up when I get really peculiar, and then, even if Charles and Marion don't put me into a mental home, they'll be able to do what they like with me. They'll put me into a home of some sort, and everyone will say how wonderfully good they've always been to me. But they won't be able to afford a really nice home where I'd be comfortable and well looked after, unless they've got control of my money, and so I want to be sure that the person who's got it is someone I trust. So I want to be sure it's you."

I took a moment to answer. Then I said, "Why don't you trust Charles and Marion?"

"Well, Marion doesn't like me, you know," she replied. "She never has. She only came here because it was a way of giving Charles the sort of good home he likes that doesn't cost him anything. But she's very bored and she'd love to be back in her old job."

Marion had been a librarian in St. Botolph's College for several years before she married Charles and in those days had had a nice little cottage of her own in Cumnor.

Aunt Emma continued, "She thinks she could get the job back if she hadn't got me to look after, so she's going to pop me into a home the first moment she can. But even if they have control of my money and could arrange to move me into somewhere nice, it would actually be into the cheapest thing they could find, and the last years of my life, or months, or weeks, whatever it turns out to be, would be pretty wretched."

I think I was frowning.

"Then just what is it you want me to do?" I asked.

"First of all, fix up the power of attorney," she said. "You'll have to get in touch with Mr. Baybridge. He's my solicitor. Of course, he won't be in his office on a Saturday morning, but if you ring his home this evening and tell him it's urgent, I'm sure he'll come to see me tomorrow. Then as soon as that's been sorted out and you're in charge, I want you to tell Charles and Marion that they aren't needed here any more because you're going to get in a woman from an agency to look after me. I've the address of a good agency who'll send someone who'll do the shopping and the cooking and everything. It's very expensive, but after all, I can afford it—particularly as it may not be for long—and meanwhile I'll feel . . ." She paused, then continued softly, "I'll feel *safe.*"

That was the first time I started to wonder if she *was* in her right mind and fit to give me power of attorney. Whereas it should have been the time when I began to take her seriously . . .

"Very well," I said, "if you're sure it's what you want. It'll be a little hard on Charles and Marion, suddenly being turned out, but I suppose they'll be able to find lodgings till they can buy a place of their own. And the first step you want me to take is to ring up Mr. Baybridge this evening and ask him to call on you here to fix up this power of attorney thing."

She nodded. "And please don't tell Charles and Marion about any of this. I know you think I'm being ungrateful, but really . . . really, Dorothy . . ."

She did not finish the sentence, and it was only later that I guessed what she had nearly said.

The telephone was on a table in the hall at the bottom of the stairs. I found Mr. Baybridge's number in a notebook beside the telephone, rang him up, and arranged with him that he should call on my aunt next morning at eleven o'clock. I did not say anything about why she wanted to see him, but only that she would be very grateful if he would come. But the door of the drawing room where Marion and Charles were sitting was open, and as I joined them, Charles said, "So she's going to change her will."

"Change her will?" I said. "She hasn't said anything about that to me."

"Isn't that why she wants Baybridge to come round?"

"Not that I know of."

Aunt Emma's will, to the best of my knowledge, left everything she had divided equally between Marion and me. It seemed to me very unlikely that she should think of changing it.

"Of course, if she did, we could contest it," Charles went on. "I think Dr. Summers would be willing to say that the balance of her mind wasn't all that it should be at the time she did it. Then we might add—" He paused and gave me one of the odd brilliant smiles that could transform his rather nondescript face into one which, at least to me, had always been surprisingly exciting. "We could talk about undue influence, couldn't we? I mean, in view of the time you've spent with her this evening."

"She never mentioned her will all the time I was with her and neither did I," I answered truthfully.

"Anyway, there's nothing wrong with the balance of her mind," Marion said. "She's old, that's all, and it happens she doesn't like you and me, Charles. I don't know why, but it's her right, isn't it? I hope no one thinks my mind is unhinged simply because I dislike some of the people I do."

I said something I was later to regret.

"*I* don't think her mind is unhinged, but she's afraid it's going to be."

Charles gave me a sombre look. "Is that really true? It hadn't occurred to me."

I remembered that Aunt Emma had said that she did not think that Charles and Marion had noticed her black-outs and other peculiarities.

Trying to make amends to her, I said, "Oh, I don't know. I expect it's just the after-effects of her stroke. She's more helpless than she's ever been in her life and she can't come to terms with it."

"All the same, you think she's afraid—" He checked himself and exchanged a long look with Marion which made me wonder if, in spite of his having said otherwise, the two of them might not already have discussed it.

Feeling guilty, as if I had somehow let Aunt Emma down, I said good night to them and went to bed.

Next morning I was awakened by Marion, who came into my room with a pot of tea on a tray. As she put it down on the table by my bed, I said, "This is very nice of you. You shouldn't have bothered."

"It's no bother. I always do it for Aunt Emma," she replied. "Come down when you feel like it. You'll probably find me in the kitchen."

"I think I'd like a bath," I said. "Does anyone else want the bathroom?"

"No, go ahead when you like." She turned to the door.

Sitting up, reaching for the tray and balancing it on my knees, I said, "Marion, last night before I went to sleep I started thinking about the things we'd been talking about. Honestly, Aunt Emma never said anything to me about changing her will. I'd a feeling you and Charles didn't believe me when I told you that."

She gave a shrug of her shoulders. I was sure I saw disbelief in her eyes. But she said, "It wouldn't break my heart if she did change it. What I want is to get back to my job. I don't think I'm cut out to be a nurse, any more than you are. But you've been lucky—no one's ever suggested you ought to give up that job of yours to do the sort of things I've had to do recently. You've always got away with everything you wanted."

Except, I thought, marrying Charles, which was something that at one time I had wanted very badly.

"But you're fond of Aunt Emma, aren't you?" I said. "She's always been very good to us both."

"Oh yes, of course," she answered indifferently. "But I'm no more domesticated than you are, you know. I can't cook and I'm not nearly as good as you are at entertaining people, which is something Charles would like me to do, and doing the shopping and being shut up half the time in this great house bores me beyond words. However, I'm sorry, I didn't mean to start grumbling so early in the morning. It's usually something that works up gradually through the day, if I've got a sympathetic listener. I'll give you a dose of it later!"

She went out, and I heard her go downstairs.

I drank my tea, then got out of bed, put on my dressing-gown, collected my sponge and toothbrush, and went to the bathroom.

I ran a deep bath, washed lazily, and lay comfortably back in the warm water, thinking how strange it was to discover that Marion's life, which I had always to some extent envied, should apparently to her be a kind of trap. I did not believe that Aunt Emma's money was unimportant to her and Charles. If it were, why had they not moved out long ago and left Aunt Emma to find herself a good housekeeper? The truth was, I thought, that Marion was one of those people who want to have everything without giving up anything to achieve it. She wanted marriage and her job and more money than she could earn at it and a luxurious home to live in . . .

It was at that point that I heard the shout or the scream or whatever the dreadful noise was, and Marion's voice crying out distinctly, "Don't! Don't!"

Then I heard a shot.

I jumped out of the bath, grabbed my dressing-gown, and, still struggling into it, ran out on to the landing. A draught from an open window sent a chill over my wet body. The door of Aunt Emma's bedroom was open. I entered.

What I saw gave me the worst shock of my life. Aunt Emma was lying in her bed with half of her head blown away. Her pillows were a mass of blood. One of her eyes seemed to have come adrift and was hanging half out of its socket. There was a strange smell in the room which I did not recognise, because I had never before been on the spot when a gun had just gone off. A revolver or an automatic pistol or whatever it was, was lying on the floor just beside the bed and one of her hands hung down over the edge of the bed, almost touching the gun. Marion was in the middle of the room shrieking.

Perhaps the right thing to have done would have been to slap her face. One reads that that is the thing to do with a case of hysterics. But I was very near shrieking myself, so without even knowing what I was doing, I wasted a moment fumbling with the zip of my dressing-gown—though even when I had dragged it shut, I found myself shivering inside it. However, when I was no longer half-naked, I felt more able to cope with things, and I took hold of Marion by the shoulders and shook her. Actually, by then she had stopped shrieking and was simply standing there shaking.

"What happened?" I yelled at her. "For God's sake, what happened?"

"I couldn't stop her," she answered frantically. "I shouted at her not to do it, but I was too late. I shouted, 'Don't!' but she went ahead and pulled the trigger. I saw her do it, Dorothy, I *saw* her. I came in, bringing her the tea, and there she was, holding the gun to her head. And it was as if she didn't know I was there. She didn't even look at me. She just pulled the trigger . . . Oh . . . Oh . . ."

I thought the shrieking was going to start again, but she only took a few steps away from the bed, dropped into a chair, and hid her face in her hands.

I saw the tea-tray where she had put it down on the table next to the bed.

"Where did the gun come from?" I asked. "Do you know?"

"I think it must be one Uncle Bertram brought back from the war," Marion answered. "I've heard her speak of it, though I don't know where she kept it."

"But why . . . why should she do it? When we talked yesterday evening, she . . . well . . . she had other plans."

Marion dropped her hands. "Wasn't she afraid of going mad? That's what you said yourself. And isn't that a good reason for killing oneself?"

At that moment Charles came into the room.

When he saw Aunt Emma and the blood and the gun and the dreadful displaced eye, he exclaimed something that sounded like, "Oh my Christ!" but it was in a hoarse, muffled tone and might have been anything. His face had gone a strange grey-white. Turning to Marion, he asked her almost exactly the same questions as I had just asked her, and she gave him the same answer, though her voice was steadier now. But she kept her eyes shut, as if she could not bear to look at the thing on the bed.

"You really saw her do it?" he asked. "You'll swear to that?"

"Of course I will . . . but why should I have to?" she asked.

"Because there'll be an inquest and you'll have to do it then," he answered. "I'm going to phone Summers now, and then— there's no point in putting it off—I'll phone the police."

Dr. Summers had been Aunt Emma's doctor for about the last ten years. She had regarded him with some distrust as a not very responsible young man, though he was well into his fifties and had several grown-up children. She used to talk wistfully of a

Dr. Charters, who had been nearly as old as she was. But young and irresponsible or not, Dr. Summers would not have much difficulty in diagnosing the cause of her death.

Marion stood up. She looked at me.

"Why don't you go and get dressed?" she said, and it was astonishing how calm she sounded. "We're going to have plenty of company presently and it may not be convenient to do it then."

It seemed good sense, so I went to my bedroom.

I heard Charles go downstairs and the tinkle of the telephone bell as he started dialling, first, I supposed, the doctor, and then the police. Presently, as I was combing my hair in front of the mirror, I smelt coffee and realised that Marion must have gone downstairs too, and I felt very glad that she had thought of it. Coffee was just what I wanted then. Yet I did not go down immediately.

Something was nagging at my mind, something about that room where Aunt Emma lay dead, something that was trying to surface in my thoughts, something that did not make sense.

I found the door of her bedroom closed and I opened it softly, as if I were afraid of disturbing her or perhaps someone else who might be in there. But of course there was no one and everything was just as it had been when I had been in the room before. But was it really just the same? Why did I feel that something had altered?

I am not sure how long I stood there, gazing at the desolate room that already had the smell of blood in it, before I realised what had changed. It was the tea-tray. When I had first burst into the room to find Marion in the middle of it screaming, the tea-tray had been on the table beside the bed. But now the tray was no longer there. Apparently Marion had taken it down to the kitchen to wash the teapot. It seemed an odd thing to have done at a time like this, but then it is just at such times that people do do very odd things, dictated simply by habit. Probably Marion had not even been aware of what she was doing.

Then I saw that she had not taken the tray downstairs. It was on a chest of drawers, just inside the door.

So far as I could tell, nothing else in the room had been moved. The gun still lay on the carpet beside the bed. Aunt Emma's dead hand dangled above it. But the tray, with a small silver teapot on it, a milk-jug, a cup and saucer, and a plate with two biscuits on it, had mysteriously been moved from the bedside table to the chest of drawers by the door.

I solved the mystery of why it had happened quite soon, though it seemed to me a long time that I stood there thinking about it. But when I went downstairs, the coffee was only just ready, so I could not have stayed in Aunt Emma's room for more than a few minutes. We drank the coffee in the kitchen, waiting for the doctor's ring at the doorbell. It came after about a quarter of an hour, and when he had taken one look at Aunt Emma's body, the only thing he said was, "You've phoned the police, of course."

"Of course," Charles answered.

We all went downstairs again, and Marion gave Dr. Summers some coffee.

Sipping it, he said thoughtfully, "I suppose we ought to have expected something like this. She seemed to get over that stroke very well, but I've realised she was depressed, not at all the high-spirited person she used to be. But I'm surprised that she shot herself. I'd have expected an overdose of the pills I've been giving her. They're fairly harmless, but if you took enough of them, they might do the job. Did you know she'd a gun?"

"Yes, I was telling my sister about it," Marion said. "I think it was a souvenir my granduncle brought back from the war. I've heard my aunt speak of it. But I didn't know where she kept it or that she'd any ammunition for it. The reason she did it— well, something my sister told us yesterday evening makes us fairly sure she'd a belief she might be going insane. And perhaps she was, though my husband and I hadn't noticed anything particularly strange about her. Some depression, yes, but she always seemed to be completely on the spot when one talked to her."

"The insane, though that isn't the fashionable word for them nowadays, can be remarkably cunning at concealing their peculiarities from the people round them," the doctor responded.

"But I don't expect there'll be any difficulties at the inquest. If you know she'd that fear in her mind, it gave her a good reason for doing what she did."

The police arrived only a few minutes later.

A shortish, stolid-looking man in plain clothes who introduced himself as Detective Inspector Foskin was in charge, and a uniformed sergeant and a constable were with him. Charles and Dr. Summers took the three men up to Aunt Emma's room while Marion and I waited in the drawing room below, listening for sounds from upstairs. But after the first tramping about there was a remarkable silence.

Then one of the men came down and used the telephone in the hall. I thought he would be ringing for an ambulance, but it seemed to be a call to the police station, asking for a photographer to be sent, as well as someone connected with fingerprints. I heard Marion let out a long breath. She was standing rigidly in front of the fireplace, where the ashes from yesterday's fire were still in a heap. A woman who cleaned the house and cleared the grate and laid a new fire, came in on most mornings, but not on a Saturday.

The sergeant, who had been telephoning, entered the drawing room and said that Inspector Foskin would be glad if Marion and I would join him upstairs and tell him exactly what had happened that morning.

We went up, the sergeant following us, and into the bedroom.

I heard Marion give a little gasp of shock. It did not surprise me. The tea-tray, which had been on the chest of drawers by the door when she had left the room, was now back on the bedside table where it had been when I had first entered the room that morning.

Inspector Foskin seemed very interested in it.

"I understand from your husband," he said to Marion, "that it was you who discovered the body this morning. Would you mind telling me exactly what happened?"

She stood there, staring at the tea-tray. Then she turned and gave me a long look. Then she turned back to the inspector.

"I came in, as I usually do, about a quarter to eight," she said.

"I brought my aunt her tea, as I did every morning, and I saw her with the gun at her head. I think I shouted, 'Don't!' or something like that, and I ran across the room to her, but before I got to her bedside she'd pulled the trigger. And I believe I started screaming. I'm not really sure what I did. The next thing I remember clearly is my sister shaking me and asking what had happened."

"But the tray you were carrying," the detective said in his stolid way. "What did you do with it?"

"The tray?" she repeated stupidly, as if she did not know what he was talking about, although her attention had been on it ever since she and I had come into the room. "I don't know. I suppose I put it down somewhere."

"Here on this table," he said, pointing. "Although you saw your aunt with a gun at her head, you carried the tray across the room and round the foot of the bed and you put it down here and only then started screaming. I find that very hard to envisage. If you'd simply dropped the whole works on the floor or put it down on the nearest thing you could—that chest of drawers by the door, for instance—I could understand it and I should probably believe your story. As it is, I'm inclined to believe it may have been you who pulled the trigger *after* you'd put the tray down on this table."

Marion's eyes met mine again. I suppose she was thinking of the time, while she had been making coffee, that I had had to myself, getting dressed and then no doubt returning to this room and putting the tray back where I had seen it when I first came into the room. Believing that she had rectified her error of leaving it on the bedside table before she killed Aunt Emma, she had been feeling reasonably safe. And so she might still have been if she had kept her head, if she had not turned on me and tried to scratch my eyes out with her nails! The evidence against her was actually very scanty.

But she was not really the type to attempt murder, any more than I am myself. I went so far as to deny that I had touched the tray, and as I had been very careful to leave no fingerprints on it I was believed. In the end, after another attack of shrieking, she broke down completely and confessed that she had killed Aunt Emma. To the end she believed that Aunt Emma had been about to change her will, cutting her and Charles out of it.

She was sentenced to life.

But of course a life sentence does not literally mean for life and the years have been passing. Charles and I have been living together for a long time now, but I am not quite sure what will happen when Marion is released from prison. I think he is happy with me. I gave up my job long ago, and we live in the old house in Elwell Street. We have plenty of money and entertain a good deal, which he enjoys. But the scandal of the murder did him a fair amount of damage, and he never obtained the professorship that he would have liked.

I still do not know for certain if he was involved in the shooting of my aunt or if the whole guilt was Marion's, and I do not like to dig too deep. She never said anything to incriminate him, but perhaps, as his wife, she would not have been able to do so. However, he has always claimed that he really did not know what she intended to do that morning when she went downstairs to make the tea. All the same, sometimes I see him looking at me in a way that makes me wonder about the future . . .

The Jackal and the Tiger

Michael Gilbert

On the evening of April 15, 1944, Colonel Hubert of Military Intelligence said to the director of public prosecutions, "The only mistake Karl made was to underestimate young Ronnie Kavanagh."

That afternoon, Karl Muller, who sometimes called himself Charles Miller, had been shot in the underground rifle-range at the Tower of London, which was the place being used at that time for the execution of German spies.

"A fatal mistake," agreed the Director.

Jim Perrot, late of the Military Police, wrote to his friend, Fred Denniston:

Dear Denny,

Do you remember those plans we talked over so often in North Africa and Italy? Well, I've got an option on a twenty-one-year lease of a nice first-floor office in Chancery Lane. That's bang in the middle of legal London, where the legal eagles are beginning to flap their wings and sharpen their claws again. Lots of work for an enquiry agency and not much competition—as yet. The lease is a snip. I've commuted my pension and got me a bit of capital. I reckon we'll have to put in about £2000 each to get going. "Denny's Detectives"! How about it?

And Denny's Detectives had turned out to be a success from the start.

As Perrot had said, there was no lack of work. Much of it was divorce work, the sad by-product of a long war. It was in connection with this branch of their activities, which neither of the partners liked, that they acquired Mr. Huffin. He was perfectly equipped for the role he had to play. He was small, mild-looking, and so insignificant that many businessmen, departing to alleged conferences in the Midlands, had failed to recognise the little man who travelled in the train with them and occupied a table in an obscure corner of their hotel dining room, until he stood up in court and swore to tell the truth, the whole truth and nothing but the truth about the lady who had shared the businessman's table and later his bedroom.

Jim Perrot's job was the tracing of elusive debtors. His experience as a policeman was useful to him here. Fred Denniston, for his part, rarely left the office. His speciality was estimating the credit-worthiness of companies. He gradually became expert at reading between the lines of optimistic profit-and-loss accounts and precariously balanced balance sheets. He developed, with experience, a quite uncanny instinct for overvalued stocks and underdepreciated assets. Perrot would sometimes see him holding a suspect document delicately between his fingers and sniffing at it, as though he could detect by smell alone the odour of falsification.

One factor that helped them to show a steady profit was their absurdly small rent. When Perrot had described the lease as a "snip" he was not exaggerating. At the end of the war, when no one was bothered about inflation, twenty-one-year leases could be had without the periodical reviews which are commonplace today. As the end of their lease approached, the partners did become aware that they were paying a good deal less than the market rent. Indeed, they could hardly help being aware of it. Their landlords, the Scotus Property Company, commented on it with increasing bitterness.

"It's no good complaining about it," said Perrot genially.

"You should have thought about that when you granted the lease."

"Just you wait till the end of the next year," said Scotus.

Denniston said, "I suppose we shall have to pay a bit more. Anyway, they can't turn us out. We're protected tenants."

When a friendly valuer from the other end of Chancery Lane learnt what their rent was, he struggled to control his feelings. "I suppose you realise," he said, "that you're paying a pound a square foot?"

"Just about what I made it," said Denniston.

"And that the going rate in this area is between five and six pounds?"

"You mean," said Perrot, "that when our lease comes to an end we'll have to pay five times the present rent?"

"Oh, at least that," said the valuer cheerfully. "But I imagine you've been putting aside a fund to meet it."

The partners looked at each other. They were well aware that they had been doing nothing of the sort.

That was the first shock.

The second was Perrot's death. He had been putting on weight and smoking too much, but had looked healthy enough. One afternoon he complained of not feeling well, went home early, and died that night.

Denniston had been fond of him, and his first feelings were of personal loss. His next feeling was that he was going to need another partner and additional capital, and that fairly quickly.

He considered, and rejected, the idea of inviting Mr. Huffin to become a partner. The main drawback was that he disliked him. And he was so totally negative. He crept into the office every morning on the stroke of nine and, unless he had some outside business, stayed in his room, which had been partitioned off from Denniston's, until half past five. The partition was so thin that he could hear him every time he got up from his chair.

"Not partner material," said Denniston to himself.

He tried advertising, but soon found that the limited number of applicants who had capital would have been unsuitable as partners, while the rather greater number, who might have been acceptable as partners, had no capital.

After some months of fruitless effort, he realised two other things. The first was that they were losing business. Jim Perrot's clients were taking their affairs elsewhere. The second was that the day of reckoning with his landlords was looming.

It was at this point that Andrew Gurney turned up. Denniston liked him at sight. He was young. He was cheerful. He seemed anxious to learn the business. And he made a proposal.

In about a year's time, when he attained the ripe old age of twenty-five, he would be coming into a bit of capital under a family trust. By that time he would have a fair idea whether the business suited him and he suited them. All being well, he was prepared to invest that capital in the firm.

They discussed amounts and dates, and came to a tentative agreement. Gurney took over Perrot's old room. Denniston breathed a sigh of relief and turned his mind to the analysis of a complex set of group accounts.

It was almost exactly a month later when Mr.Huffin knocked on his door, put his head round, blinked twice, and said, "If you're not too busy, I wonder if I might have a word with you?"

"I'm doing nothing that can't wait," replied Denniston.

Mr. Huffin slid into the room, advanced towards the desk, and then, as if changing his mind at the last moment, seated himself in the chair that was normally reserved for clients.

Denniston was conscious of a slight feeling of surprise. Previously when Mr. Huffin had come to see him, he had stood in front of the desk and had waited, if the discussion was likely to be lengthy, for an invitation to sit down.

He was even more surprised when Mr. Huffin spoke. He said, "You're in trouble, aren't you?"

It was not only that Mr. Huffin had omitted the "sir" which he had previously used when addressing his employer. It was more than that. There was something sharp and cold in the tone of his voice. It was like the sudden unexpected chill which announces the end of autumn and the beginning of winter.

"You haven't seen fit to take me into your confidence," Mr.

Huffin continued, "but the wall between our offices is so thin that it's impossible for me not to hear every word that's said."

Denniston had recovered himself sufficiently to say, "The fact that you can overhear confidential matters doesn't entitle you to trade on them."

"When the ship's sinking," said Mr. Huffin, "etiquette has to go by the board."

This was followed by a silence which Denniston found it difficult to break. In the end he said, "It's true that Mr. Perrot's death has left us in a difficult position. But, as it happens, I have been able to make arrangements which should tide us over."

"You mean young Gurney? In the month he's been here he's earned less than half you pay him. And speaking personally, I should have said that he's got no real aptitude for the work. What you need is someone without such nice manners, but with a thicker skin."

Denniston said, "Look here, Mr. Huffin—" and stopped. He was on the point of saying, "If you don't like the way I run this firm, we can do without you."

But could they?

As though reading his thoughts Mr. Huffin said, "In the old days, Mr. Perrot, you, and I earned roughly equal amounts. Recently the proportions have been slipping. Last year I brought in half our fees. At least those were the figures you gave our auditor, so I assume they're correct."

"You listened to that discussion also?"

"I felt I was an interested party."

Mr. Denniston said, "All right. I accept that your services have been valuable. If that's your point, you've made it. I imagine it's leading up to something else. You want an increase in salary?"

"Not really."

"Then perhaps you had it in mind that I should make you a partner?"

"Not exactly—"

"Then . . . ?"

"My proposal was that I should take over the firm."

In the long silence that followed, Denniston found himself revising his opinion of Mr. Huffin. His surface meekness was, he realised, a piece of professional camouflage; as meaningless as the wigs of the barristers or the pin-striped trousers of the solicitors.

Mr. Huffin continued, "Have you thought out what would happen if I did leave? Maybe you could make enough to cover expenses. Until your lease expires. But what then? Have you, I wonder, overlooked one point? At the conclusion of a twenty-one-year lease, there is bound to be a heavy bill for dilapidations."

"Dilapidations?" Denniston repeated slowly. The five syllables chimed together in an ominous chord. "Surely there's nothing much to do?"

"I took the precaution of having a word with an old friend, a Mr. Ellen. He's one of the surveyors used by the Scotus Property Company. He's a leading expert in his field and his calculations are very rarely challenged by the Court. Last weekend I arranged for him to make an inspection. He thought that the cost of carrying out all the necessary work, in a first-class fashion, would be between six thousand pounds and eight thousand pounds."

"For God's sake!" said Denniston. "It can't be."

"He showed me the breakdown. It could be more."

To give himself time to think, Denniston said very slowly, "If you have such a poor opinion of the prospects of the firm, why would you want to buy me out?"

"I'm sorry," said Mr. Huffin gently. "You've misunderstood me. I wasn't proposing to pay you anything. After all, what have you got to sell?"

It was not Denniston's habit to discuss business with his wife. But this was a crisis. He poured out the whole matter to her as soon as he got home that evening.

"And I know damned well what he'll do," he said. "As soon as he's got me out, he'll bring in some accomplice of his own. They won't stick to divorce work. That's legal at least. The real money's in dirty work. Finding useful witnesses and bribing them to say what your client wants. Faking evidence. Fudging expert reports."

"He seems to be prepared to pay eight thousand pounds for the privilege of doing it," his wife replied.

"Of course he won't. That's a put-up job between him and his old pal Mr. Ellen of Scotus. He'll pay a lot less and be allowed to pay it in easy instalments."

"What happens if you say no?"

"I'd have to challenge the dilapidations. It'd mean going to court and that's expensive."

"If you used some of Gurney's money—" Mrs. Denniston stopped.

They were both straightforward people. Denniston put what she was thinking into words: "I can't take that boy's money and put it into a legal wrangle."

"And there's no other way of raising it?"

"None that I can think of."

"Then that's that," said his wife. "I'd say, cut your losses and clear out. We're still solvent. We'll think of something to do."

It took a lot of talk to persuade him, but in the end he saw the force of her arguments. "All right," he said. "No sense in dragging it out. I'll go in tomorrow and tell Huffin he can have the firm. I'll also tell him what I think of him."

"It won't do any good."

"It'll do me a lot of good."

On the following evening he arrived back on the stroke of six. He kissed his wife and said to her, "Whatever you were thinking of cooking for supper, think again. We're going out to find the best dinner London can provide. We'll drink champagne before it, burgundy with it, and brandy after it."

His wife, who had spent the day worrying about how they were going to survive, said, "Really Fred. Do you think we ought—"

"Certainly we ought. We're celebrating."

"Celebrating what?"

"A miracle!"

It had happened at nine o'clock that morning. Whilst Denniston was polishing up the precise terms in which he intended to say goodbye to Mr. Huffin, his secretary came into his room. She was looking ruffled. She said, "Could you be free to see Mr. Kavanagh at ten?"

Denniston looked at his diary and said, "Yes. That'll be all right. Who is Mr. Kavanagh?"

"Mr. Ronald Kavanagh," said his secretary. As he was still looking blank she added, "Kavanagh Lewisohn and Fitch. He's the chairman."

"Good God! How do you know that?" Denniston enquired.

"Before I came here, I worked in their head office."

"Do you know Mr. Kavanagh?"

"I was in the typing pool. I caught a glimpse of him twice in the three years I was there."

"Did he say what he wanted?"

"He wanted to see you."

"You're sure he didn't ask me to go and see him? He's coming here?"

"That's what he said."

"It must be some mistake," said Denniston.

Kavanagh Lewisohn and Fitch were so well known that people said KLF and assumed you would understand what they meant. They were one of the largest credit sale firms in London —so large that they rarely dealt with individual customers. They sold everything from computer banks to motor cars and from television sets to washing machines to middlemen, who, in turn, sold them to retailers. If Ronald Kavanagh was really planning to visit a small firm of enquiry agents, it could hardly be in connection with business matters. It must be private trouble. Something that needed to be dealt with discreetly.

When Kavanagh arrived, he turned out to be a slight, quiet, unassuming person in his early fifties. Denniston was agreeably surprised. Such managing directors of large companies as he had come across in the past had been intimidating people, assertive of their status and conscious of their financial muscle. A further surprise was that he really had come to talk business.

He said, "This is something I wanted to deal with myself. Some time ago you did credit-rating reports for us on two potential customers." He mentioned their names.

"Yes," said Denniston, wondering what had gone wrong.

"We were impressed by the thorough way you tackled them. I assume, by the way, that you did the work yourself?"

Denniston nodded.

"You gave a good rating to one, although it was a new company. The other, which was older and apparently sound, you warned us against. In both cases you were absolutely right. That's why I'm here today. Up to the present we've been getting the reports we needed from half a dozen different sources. This is now such an important part of our business that the board has decided that it would like to concentrate it in one pair of hands. Our first idea was to offer you the work on a retainer basis. Then we had a better idea." Mr. Kavanagh smiled. "We decided to buy you. That is, of course, if you're for sale?"

Denniston was incapable of speech.

"We had it in mind to purchase your business as a going concern. We would take over the premises as they stand. There is, however, one condition. It's *your* brains and *your* flair that we're buying. We should have to ask you to enter into a service contract, at a fair salary, for five years certain, with options on both sides to renew. Your existing staff too, if they wish. But you are the one we must have."

The room, which had shown signs of revolving on its axis, slowed down. Denniston took a grip of himself. He said, "Your offer is more than fair, but there is one thing you ought to know. You spoke of taking over these premises. There is a snag . . ."

When Denniston had finished, Kavanagh said, "It was good of you to tell me. It accords, if I may say so, with your reputation. We are not unacquainted with Scotus." He smiled gently. "We had some dealings with them over one of our branch offices last year. Fortunately we have very good solicitors and excellent surveyors. The outcome was a lot happier for us than it was for them. However, in this case it doesn't arise. Our own service department will carry out such repairs and redecoration as *we* consider necessary. If Scotus object, they can take us to court. I don't think they will. They're timid folk when they're up against someone bigger than themselves."

"Like all bullies," said Denniston. As he said it, he reflected with pleasure that Mr. Huffin had undoubtedly got his ear glued to the wall.

It soon became apparent that Ronald Kavanagh was not a man who delegated to others things that he enjoyed doing himself.

On the morning after the deal had been signed he limped into the room, accompanied by the head of his service department and a foreman. They inspected everything and made notes. The next morning, a gang of workmen arrived and started to turn the office upside down.

Kavanagh arrived with the workmen. He said to Denniston, "We'll start with your room. Strip and paint the whole place. They can do it in two days. What colours do you fancy?"

"Something cheerful."

"I agree. My solicitor's office looks as if it hasn't been dusted since Charles Dickens worked there. What we want is an impression of cheerful reliability. Cream paint, venetian blinds, and solid-brass light fittings. And we'll need a second desk. I propose to establish a niche here for myself. I hope you don't mind?"

"I don't mind at all," said Denniston. It occurred to him that one cause of his depression had been that since Perrot's death he had really had no one to talk to. "I'll be glad of your company, though I don't suppose you'll be able to spare us a lot of time."

"It's a common fallacy," said Kavanagh, sitting on a corner of the table, swinging his damaged leg ("a relic of war service," he explained), "widely believed, but quite untrue, that managing directors are busy men. If they are, it's a sign of incompetence. I have excellent subordinates who do the real work. All I have to do is utter occasional sounds of approval or disapproval. It's such a boring life that a new venture like this is a breath of fresh air. Oh, you want to move this table. We'd better shift into young Gurney's office."

"As I was saying," Kavanagh continued when they had established themselves in Gurney's room, "I have an insatiable curiosity about the mechanics of other people's business. When we went into the second-hand car market, we took over a motor-repair outfit. I got so interested that I put on overalls and started to work there myself. The men thought it was a huge joke, but they soon got used to it. And the things I learnt about faking repair bills, you wouldn't believe. Oh, sorry, I'm afraid they want to start work in here too. Let's go to my club and get ourselves an early luncheon."

Denniston found the new regime very pleasant. Kavanagh did not, of course, spend all his time with them, but he managed to put in a full hour on most days. His method of working was to have copies made, on the modern photocopying machine which had been one of his first innovations, of all of Denniston's reports. These he would study carefully, occasionally asking for the working papers. The questions he asked were shrewd and could not be answered without thought.

"Really," he said, "we're in the same line of business. Success depends on finding out who to trust. I once turned down a prosperous-looking television wholesaler because he turned up in a Green Jackets' tie. I'm damned certain he'd never been near the brigade. Quite the wrong shape for a rifleman."

"Instinct, based on experience," agreed Denniston. He already felt years younger. It was not only the steady flow of new work and the certainty of getting a cheque at the end of each month. The whole office seemed to have changed. Even Mr. Huffin appeared to be happy. Not only had his room been repainted, but it had been furnished with a new desk and a set of gleaming filing cabinets equipped with Chubb locks. These innovations seemed to have compensated him for the setback to his own plans, and he went out of his way to be pleasant to Kavanagh when he encountered him.

"Slimy toad," said Denniston to his wife. "When I asked Kavanagh if he planned to keep him, he laughed and said, 'Why not? I don't much like the sort of work he's doing, but it brings in good money. As long as he keeps within the law. If you hear any complaints of sharp practice, that's another matter.'"

"He sounds terrific."

"Terrific's not quite the right word. He's honest, sensible, and unassuming. Also he's still a bit of a schoolboy. He likes to see the wheels go round."

"I don't believe a single word of it," said his wife.

"Well, Uncle," said Andrew Gurney. "What next?"

Kavanagh said, "Next, I think, a glass of port."

"Then it must be something damned unpleasant," said Gurney.

"Why?"

"If it wasn't, you wouldn't be wasting the club port on me."

"You're an irreverent brat," said Kavanagh.

"When you wangled me into the firm, I guessed you were up to something."

"Two large ports, please, Barker. Actually all I want you to do is to commit a burglary."

"I said it was going to be something unpleasant."

"But this is a very safe burglary. You are to burgle the offices of Denny's Detectives. Since the firm belongs to me, technically hardly a burglary at all, wouldn't you say?"

"Well . . ." said Gurney cautiously.

"I will supply you with the key of the outer door, the key of Mr. Huffin's room, and a key for each of his new filing cabinets and his desk. Mr. Huffin is a careful man. When these were installed, he asked for the duplicate keys to be handed to him. Fortunately I had had a second copy made of each. Nevertheless, I was much encouraged by his request. It showed me that I might be on the right track."

"What track?"

Kavanagh took a sip of his port and said, "It's Warre '63. Don't gulp it. I suggest that you start around eleven o'clock. By that time Chancery Lane should be deserted except for the occasional policeman. In case you should run into trouble, I'll supply you with a note stating that you are working late with my permission."

"Yes, Uncle, but—"

"When you get into Mr. Huffin's room, take all the files from his cabinets and all the papers from his desk and photocopy them. Be very careful to put them back in the order you found them."

"Yes, but—"

"I don't imagine you'll be able to finish the job in one night or even in two. When you leave, bring the photocopies round to my flat. You can use my spare room and make up for your lost nights by sleeping by day. I'll warn my housekeeper. As far as the office is concerned, you're out of town on a job for me. I think that's all quite straightforward."

"Oh, quite," said Gurney. "The only thing is you haven't told me what you're up to."

"When I've had a chance of examining Mr. Huffin's papers, I may have a clearer idea myself. As soon as I do, I'll put you in the picture."

Andrew sighed. "When do you want me to start?"

"It's Monday today. If you start tomorrow night you should be through by the end of the week. I suggest you go home now and get a good night's rest."

As his uncle had predicted, it took Andrew exactly four nights to finish the job. If he expected something dramatic to happen, he was disappointed. For a week his uncle failed to turn up at the office.

"Our owner," said Mr. Huffin, with a smirk, "seems to have lost interest in us."

Andrew smiled and agreed. He had just had an invitation to dinner at his uncle's flat in Albany and guessed that things might be moving.

During dinner his uncle spoke only of cricket. He was a devotee of the Kent team, most of whom he seemed to know by name. After dinner, which was cooked and served by the housekeeper, they retired to the sitting room. Kavanagh said, "And how did you enjoy your experience as a burglar?"

"It was a bit creepy at first. Chancery Lane seems to be inhabited after nightfall by howling cats."

"They're not cats. They're the spirits of disappointed litigants."

"Did I produce whatever it was you were looking for?"

"The papers from the cabinets related only to Mr. Huffin's routine work. They showed him to be a thorough, if somewhat unscrupulous, operator. A model truffle-hound. Ninety-nine percent of his private papers likewise. But the other one percent— two memoranda and a bundle of receipts—were worth all the rest put together. They demonstrated that Mr. Huffin has a second job. He's a moonlighter."

"He's crooked enough for anything. What's his other job? Some sort of blackmail I suppose."

"Try not to use words loosely, Andrew. Blackmail has become a portmanteau word covering everything from illegal intimidation to the use of lawful leverage."

"I can't imagine Mr. Huffin intimidating anyone."

"Personally, probably not. But he has a partner. And that man we must now locate. Those scraps of paper are his footprints."

Andrew looked at his uncle. He knew something of the work he had done during the war, but he found it hard to visualise this mild grey-haired man pursuing, in peace, the tactics which had brought Karl Muller and others to the rifle-range in the Tower. For the first time he was striking the flint under the topsoil and it was a curiously disturbing experience.

He said, "You promised—"

"Yes, I promised. So be it. Does the name David Rogerson mean anything to you?"

"I knew he was one of your friends."

"More than that. During the retreat to Dunkirk he managed to extract me from a crashed and burning lorry. Which was, incidentally, full of explosives. That was when I broke my right leg in several places and contracted a limp which ended my service as an infanteer. Which was why I went into intelligence. I kept up with David after the war. Not as closely as I should have liked. He had married a particularly stupid woman. However, we met once or twice a year for lunch in the City. We were both busy. I was setting up KLF, and he was climbing the ladder in Clarion Insurance. About six months ago he asked me to lend him some money. He wanted a thousand pounds. Of course I said yes and didn't ask him what he wanted it for. But I suppose he felt he owed me some sort of explanation. When he was leaving, he said, with something like a smile, 'Do you play draughts?' I said I did when I was a boy. 'Well,' he said, 'I've been huffed. By Mr. Huffin.' And that was all he did say. The next news I had was of his death."

Gurney said, "I read about that. No one seemed to know why he did it."

"You may recall that at the inquest his wife was asked whether he had left a note. She said no. That was a lie. He did leave a note. As I discovered later. David had made me his executor. My first job was to look after his wife. I soon saw that Phyllis Rogerson had one objective. To live her own life on the proceeds of some substantial insurance policies which David had taken out—and to forget about him. I accepted that this was a natural reaction. Women are realists. It was when I was clearing up his papers that she told me the truth. He had left a letter. It was addressed to me. She said, 'I guessed it was something to do with the trouble he'd been having. I knew that if you read it, all the unpleasantness would have to come out into the open. So I burnt it. I didn't even read it.' I said, 'If it was some sort of blackmailer, David won't have been his only victim. He must be caught and punished.' She wouldn't listen. I haven't spoken to her since."

"But you located Mr. Huffin."

"That wasn't difficult. The Huffin clan is not large. A clergyman in Shropshire, a farmer in Wales. A maiden lady in Northumberland. Little Mr. Huffin of Denny's Detectives was so clearly the first choice that I had no hesitation in trying him first."

"Clearly enough for you to spend your company's money in buying the agency."

"We were on the lookout for a good credit-rating firm. My board was unanimous that Denniston was the man for the job.

So I was able to kill two birds with one stone. Always an agreeable thing to do. My first idea was to expose Huffin as a blackmailer. I felt that there would be enough evidence in his files to convict him. I was wrong. What those papers show is that a second man is involved. Possibly the more important villain of the two. I see Huffin as the reconnaissance unit. The other man as the heavy brigade."

"Do you know his name?"

"The only lead I have to him is that Mr. Huffin used to communicate privately with a Mr. Angus. The address he wrote to was a small newsagent's shop in Tufnell Park. An accommodation address, no doubt. Receipts for the payments he made to the shopkeeper were among his papers. I visualise Mr. Angus calling from time to time to collect his letters. Or he may send a messenger. That is something we shall have to find out."

"And you want me to watch the shop?"

"It's kind of you to offer. But no. Here I think we want professional help. Captain Smedley will be the man for the job. You've never heard of him? He's the head of a detective agency." Rather unkindly, Kavanagh added, "A *real* detective agency, Andrew."

Captain Smedley said, "I shall need exactly a hundred, in ones and fives. That's what it will cost to buy the man in the shop. I'll pay it to him myself. He won't play silly buggers with me."

Kavanagh looked at Captain Smedley, who had a face like a hank of wire rope and agreed that no one was likely to play silly buggers with him.

"I'll have a man outside. All the shopkeeper's got to do is tip him the wink when the letter's collected. Then my man follows him back to wherever he came from."

"Might it be safer to have two men outside?"

"Safer, but more expensive."

"Expense no object."

"I see," said the Captain. He looked curiously at Mr. Kavanagh, whom he had known for some time. "All right. I'll fix it up for you."

On the Wednesday of the third week following this conversation Kavanagh got a thick plain envelope addressed to him at his flat. It contained several pages of typescript, which he read carefully. The look on his face was partly enlightenment and partly disgust.

"What a game," he said. "I wonder how they work it."

After breakfast he spent some time in the reference section of the nearest public library browsing among civil service lists and copies of Whitaker's Almanack. Finally he found the name he wanted. Arnold Robbins. Yes, Arnold would certainly help him if the matter was put to him in the right way. But it would need devilish careful handling. "A jackal," he said, "and a tiger. Now all we need is a tethered goat to bring the tiger under the rifle. But it will have to be tethered very carefully, in exactly the right spot. The brute is a man-eater, no question!"

A lady touched him on the shoulder and pointed to the notice which said SILENCE, PLEASE. He was not aware that he had spoken aloud.

During the months that followed, Kavanagh resumed his regular visits to the office in Chancery Lane, but Denniston noticed that his interest in the details of the work appeared to be slackening. He would still read the current reports and comment on them, but more of his time seemed to be spent in conversation.

In the old days Denniston might have objected to this as being a waste of time which could better have been spent in earning profits. Now it was different. He was being paid a handsome salary, and if it pleased the owner of the firm to pass an occasional hour in gossip, why should he object? Moreover, Kavanagh was an excellent talker, with a rich fund of experience in the byways of the jungle which lies between Temple Bar and Aldgate Pump. Politics, economics, finance. Honesty, dishonesty, and crime. Twenty years of cut-and-thrust between armies whose soldiers wore lounge suits and carried rolled umbrellas. Warfare in which victory could be more profitable, and defeat more devastating, than on any actual field of battle.

On one occasion, Kavanagh, after what must have been an

unusually good luncheon, had devoted an entertaining hour to a
dissertation on the tax system.

"At the height of their power and arrogance," he said, "the
church demanded one-tenth of a man's income. The government
of England exacts six times as much. The pirate who sank an
occasional ship, the highwayman who held up a coach, was a
child compared to the modern taxman."

"You can't fight the state," said Denniston.

"It's been tried. Poujade in France. But I agree that massive
tax resistance is self-defeating. Each man must fight for himself.
There are lawyers and accountants who specialise in finding
loopholes in the tax laws, but such success can only be tempo-
rary. As soon as a loophole is discovered, the next finance act
shuts it up. No. The essentials of guerrilla warfare are conceal-
ment and agility."

Really interested now, Denniston said, "Have you discovered
a practical method of side-stepping tax? I've never made excessive profits, but I do resent handing over a slab of what I've
made to a government who spend most of it on vote-catching
projects."

"My method is not one which would suit everyone. Its merit
is simplicity. I arrange with my board that they will pay me only
two-thirds of what I ought to be getting. The other third goes to
charities nominated by me. They, of course, pay no tax. That
part of it is quite legitimate. Our constitution permits gifts to
charity."

"Then how—"

"The only fact which is *not* known is that I set up and control
the charities concerned. One is a local village affair. Another
looks after our own employees. A third is for members of my old
regiment. I am chairman, secretary, and treasurer of all three.
Some of the money is devoted to the proper objects of the charity. The balance comes back, by various routes, to me. A lovely
tax-free increment."

"But," said Denniston, "surely—"

"Yes?"

"It seems too simple."

"Simple, but, I assure you, effective."

And later, to himself, "I wonder if that was too obvious. I can only wait and see."

"There's something stirring," said Captain Smedley. "My men tell me that those two beauties have got a regular meeting place. Top of the Duke of York's Steps. It isn't possible to get close enough to hear what they're saying. No doubt that's why they chose it. But they're certainly worked up about something. Licking their lips, you might say."

"The bleating of the goat," said Kavanagh. "Excites the tiger."

The letter which arrived at his flat a week later was in a buff envelope, typed on buff paper. It was headed, "Inland Revenue Special Investigation Branch". It said:

Our attention has been drawn by the charity commissioners to certain apparent discrepancies in the latest accounts submitted to them of the undermentioned charities, all of which have been signed by you as treasurer. It is for this reason that we are making a direct approach to you before any further action is considered. The charities are the Lamperdown Village Hall Trust, the City of London Fusiliers' Trust, and the KLF Employees' Special Fund. You may feel that an interview would clarify the points at issue, in which case the writer would be happy to call on you, either at your place of business or at your residence, as you may prefer.

The writer appeared to be a Mr. Wagner.

Kavanagh observed with appreciation the nicely judged mixture of official suavity and concealed threat. A queen's pawn opening.

Before answering it, he had a telephone call to make. The man he was asking for was evidently important, since he had to be approached through a secretary and a personal assistant, with suitable pauses at each stage. When contact had been made, a friendly conversation ensued, conducted on Christian-name terms. It concluded with Ronnie inviting Arnold to lunch at his club on the following Monday.

He then composed a brief letter to Mr. Wagner, suggesting a meeting at his flat at seven o'clock in the evening on the following Wednesday. He apologised for suggesting such a late hour, but daytime commitments made it difficult to fix anything earlier.

"I wonder if it really is a tiger," mused Kavanagh. "Or only a second jackal. That would be disappointing."

When he opened the door to his visitor, his fears were set at rest. Mr. Wagner was a big man with a red-brown face. There was a tuft of sandy hair growing down each cheekbone. He had the broad, flattened nose of a pugilist. His eyes were so light as to be almost yellow, and a deep fold ran down under each eye to form a fence round the corners of an unusually wide mouth. His black coat was glossy, his legs decorously striped. He was a tiger. A smooth and shining tiger.

"Come in," said Kavanagh. "I'm alone this evening. Can I get you a drink?"

"Not just now," said Mr. Wagner.

He seated himself, opened his briefcase, took out a folder of papers, and laid it on the table. This was done without a word spoken. The folder was tied with tape. Mr. Wagner's spatulate fingers toyed with the tape and finally untied it. With deliberation he extracted a number of papers and arranged them in two neat lines. Kavanagh, who had also seated himself, seemed hypnotised by this methodical proceeding.

When everything was to his satisfaction, Mr. Wagner raised his heavy head, fixed his yellow eyes on Kavanagh, and said, "I'm afraid you're in trouble." An echo. Had not Mr. Huffin said the same thing?

"Trouble?"

"You're in trouble, because you've been cheating."

Kavanagh said, "Oh!" Then, sinking a little in his chair, "You've no right to say a thing like that."

"I've every right to say it, because it's true. I've been studying the accounts of the three charities I mentioned in my letter. In particular, the accounts you submitted last month. They proved interesting indeed." The voice had become a purr. "Previously your accounts were in such general terms that they might have meant—or concealed—anything. The latest accounts are, fortunately, much fuller and much more specific."

"Well," said Kavanagh, trying out a smile, "the commissioners did indicate that they wanted rather more detail as to where the money went."

"Yes, Mr. Kavanagh. And where did it go?"

"It's—" Kavanagh waved a hand feebly towards the table. "It's all there. In the accounts."

"Then shall we look at them? These are the accounts of the Fusiliers' Trust. Previously the accounts only showed a lump sum, described as 'grants to disabled Fusiliers and to the widows and dependants of deceased Fusiliers.' "

"Yes. Yes. That's right."

"In the latest accounts you supply a list of their names." The voice deepened even further. The purr became a growl. The tiger was ready to spring. "A very interesting list, because on reference to the army authorities, we have been unable to find any record of any of the people you mentioned as having served with the Fusiliers."

"Possibly—"

"Yes, Mr. Kavanagh?"

"Some mistake—"

"Thirty names. *All* of them fictitious?"

Kavanagh seemed incapable of speech.

"On the other hand, when we look at the KLF Fund, we find that the names you have given do correspond to the names of former employees of the firm. But a further question then presents itself. Have these people in fact received the sums shown against their names. Well? Well? Nothing to say? It would be very simple to find out. A letter to each of them—"

This seemed to galvanise Kavanagh into action for the first time. He half rose in his seat and said, "No. I absolutely forbid it."

"But are you in any position to forbid it?"

Kavanagh considered this question carefully, conscious that Mr. Wagner's yellow eyes were watching him. Then he said, "It does seem that there may have been some irregularity in the presentation of these accounts. I cannot attend to all these matters myself, you understand. Income may not always go where it should. There may be some tax which ought to have been paid . . ."

Mr. Wagner had begun to smile. The opening of his lips displayed a formidable set of teeth.

"I had always understood," went on Kavanagh, "that in these circumstances, if the tax was paid, together with a sum by way of penalties—"

Mr. Wagner's mouth shut with a snap. He said, "Then you misunderstood the position. It is not simply a question of payment. When you sign your tax return, the form is so arranged that if you make a deliberate misstatement you can be charged before the court with perjury."

There was a long silence. Kavanagh was thinking, "So that's how he does it. Poor old David. I wonder what slip-up he made. I'm sure it was unintentional, but a charge of perjury. Goodbye to his prospects with the Clarion. And a lot of other things too."

He said, in a voice which had become almost a bleat, "You must understand how serious that would be for me, Mr. Wagner. I'd be willing to pay any sum rather than have that happen. Is there no way . . ."

He let the sentence tail off.

Mr. Wagner had taken a silver pencil from his pocket and seemed to be making some calculations. He said, "If, in fact, the sums of money shown as going to the beneficiaries of these three trusts ended up in your own pocket, I would estimate—a rough calculation only—that you have been obtaining at least ten thousand pounds a year free of tax. I am not aware of how long this very convenient arrangement has been going on. Five years? Yes? Possibly more. Had you declared this income, you would have paid at least thirty thousand pounds of tax."

"Exactly," said Kavanagh eagerly. "That is the point I was making. Isn't this something that could more easily be solved by a money payment? At the moment I have considerable resources. If a charge of perjury was brought, they would largely disappear. What good would that do to anyone?"

Mr. Wagner appeared to consider the matter. Then he smiled. It was a terrible smile. He said, "I have some sympathy with that point of view, Mr. Kavanagh. Allow me to make a suggestion. It is a friendly suggestion. You can always refuse it. At the moment the file is entirely under my control. The information came from a private source. It is known only to me. You follow me?"

"I think so. Yes."

Mr. Wagner leaned forward and said with great deliberation, "If you will pay me ten thousand pounds, the file will be destroyed."

"Ten thousand pounds?"

"Ten thousand pounds."

"How would the payment be made?"

"You would pay the money into an account in the name of M. Angus at the Westminster branch of the London and Home Counties Bank."

"That should be enough for you," said Kavanagh. He was addressing the door leading into the next room, which now opened to admit Sir Arnold Robbins, the deputy head of Inland Revenue and two other men. Robbins said, "You are suspended from duty. These gentlemen are police officers. They will accompany you home and will impound your passport. It will be for the director of public prosecutions to decide on any further action."

Mr. Wagner was on his feet. His face was engorged. A trickle of blood ran from one nostril down his upper lip. He dashed it away with the back of his hand and said in a voice thick with fury, "So it was a trap."

"You must blame your accomplice for that," said Kavanagh. "He saw the writing on the wall and sold you to save his own skin. There's not much honour among thieves."

When Wagner had gone, Sir Arnold said, "I apologise for not believing you. I suppose the fact is we give these special-investigation people too much rope. Incidentally, I've had a look at Rogerson's file. It was as you thought. A minor omission, not even his own income. Some money his wife got from Ireland. She may not even have told him about it."

"Probably not," said Kavanagh. "She was a stupid woman." He switched off the microphone which connected with the next room. "We've got all this on tape if you need it."

"Good. And by the way, I take it those donations of yours are in order?"

"Perfectly. Every penny that went into those charities has gone to the beneficiaries. I'll show you the receipts. The only thing I fudged was that list of Fusilier names. I'll have to apologise to the charity commissioners and send them the correct list."

As Sir Arnold was going, he said, "Why did you tell Wagner it was his accomplice who had shopped him. Was it true?"

"No," said Kavanagh. "But I thought it might have some interesting results. It's going to be very difficult to get at Mr. Huffin. He really was only the jackal. He picked up scraps of information when he was doing his job and fed them to Wagner, who moved in for the kill. Wagner will be at liberty until the director makes up his mind. I felt we should give him a chance to ask Mr. Huffin for an explanation."

"He didn't say anything," said Captain Smedley. "He just hit him. Huffin's not a big man. It lifted him off his feet and sent him backwards down the steps. Cracked his skull. Dead before he got to hospital."

"And Mr. Wagner?"

"I had a policeman standing by, like you suggested. I thought he was going to put up a fight, but he seemed dazed. When they got him to the station, he just keeled over. Some sort of cerebral haemorrhage."

"So he's dead too?"

"No. But near enough. And if he does recover, he's in every sort of trouble. A good riddance to a nasty pair."

But that was not their real epitaph. That had been spoken by Colonel Hubert on the evening of April 15 in the year 1944.

Family Business

Michael Z. Lewin

1

At 0938 hours Gina heard footsteps on the stairs. She sat up from the typewriter and ran a hand through her hair. When the door opened, she was ready with businesslike attention.

In the old days the door had the words PLEASE KNOCK BEFORE ENTERING lettered at the bottom of the glass, but when Gina took over as receptionist-secretary she pointed out that nobody could come up the stairs without being heard and suggested that the door could do without being knocked on. The Old Man, of course, hadn't changed the door, but one of the first things Angelo had done was get the sign painter in to alter the lettering to NO NEED TO KNOCK BEFORE ENTERING. It was longer and that disturbed the symmetry and the Old Man didn't like it and Gina's idea had been to paint out all the stuff about knocking, but Angelo had gone one better and that was Angelo for you.

When the door opened, a woman looked hesitantly into the room.

"Hello," Gina said. "Come in."

The woman was about forty with greying brown hair. Despite the invitation, she was still uncertain. "Is this the detective agency?" she asked.

"That's right," Gina replied. "Can we help you?"

The woman looked as if she was reminding herself of a decision already made. She stepped in and closed the door carefully. Then she turned to face Gina. "Is the detective in?"

"We have a number of operatives," Gina said, "but they are all out working at the moment."

"Oh," the woman said.

"Mr. Angelo Lunghi is the head of the agency. I can ring him on his car phone if it is an emergency."

"I know all about car phones," the woman said. But it didn't sound like an emergency.

Gina said, "Perhaps the best thing is if you sit down and tell me generally what the problem is."

"You?" the woman said. Her face said, "You? The receptionist?"

"That's right. What you say to me is entirely confidential, I promise you. And although Mr. Lunghi supervises all our cases personally, I can certainly assess whether we are likely to be able to help you."

"I see," the woman said.

"As well as being receptionist and secretary here," Gina said, "I am also Mrs. Lunghi."

2

Dinner was served at 1910, the Lunghis' traditional Thursday evening meal, a hot curry made by Rosetta, Angelo's sister, whose domestic duties doubled with a part-time role as agency accountant. Thursday was a full family evening, which meant that the Old Man and Momma came down from their flat and that the two children, David and Marie, were expected to organise their school and social lives in such a way as to be there. Only Sal—Salvatore, Angelo's older brother, the painter—was not regularly there on Thursdays, Sunday afternoons, and Tuesdays. But sometimes he came and sometimes he brought one of his models, as he called them. It was not an issue.

Gina's parents lived in another city these days.

Tonight Angelo rubbed his hands together as he sat down. "Good good good," he said.

"Hey, and what's wrong with spaghetti?" the Old Man asked. But it was in a friendly way, and he said that sort of thing often. Spaghetti or some other pasta was on Sunday.

"Sorry I didn't get back to the office," Angelo said.

"We coped," Gina said.

"You know that guy Hardwick?"

They all knew that guy Hardwick, as various bits of investigation for Hardwick's solicitors had formed the major part of the agency's work for more than four weeks.

"Suddenly friend Hardwick decides that he *does* remember where he was on the night of April 18."

A groan went up from around the table.

"If he's going to be stupid enough to plead amnesia," the Old Man said, "then he ought to be smart enough to remember that he has amnesia."

Everybody laughed.

"So what came into the office today?" Angelo asked.

"We were quite busy."

"Good good good," Angelo said and rubbed his hands.

David mimicked his father a moment after. "Gooda gooda gooda."

"Smart alec," Angelo said, and swatted David on the top of the head. "Tufty smart alec."

David reconstructed his hair. It was all good-humoured.

"The main thing was a woman whose son has too much money."

"We should all have such a problem," Momma said.

"But as far as the woman can tell, the son doesn't work for it. He doesn't have a regular job and won't explain where it comes from."

Everyone was listening now. Most agency work was for solicitors or involved missing relatives or related to faithless spouses, though the Old Man had once had a murder and would only too happily tell the whole thing yet again. But a son with too much money was unusual. They began to vie gently for the chance to ask Gina questions.

Several began to speak. Angelo held up his hand and established chairmanship. "Marie."

"How old is the son?" Marie, fourteen, asked.

"Too old for you, my girl."

Marie blushed, but smiled. She enjoyed her position as the family heartbreaker.

"The boy is twenty-two," Gina said.

"And still lives at home?" Angelo asked.

"You still live at home," the Old Man said.

"Our situation is not an ordinary one," Momma said.

"That's right," David said. They all looked at him. "Our house is bigger than most people's." They laughed. A pretender for "family wit."

"Twenty-two years of age." The Old Man looked thoughtful. "So what does he do that his mother doesn't know what he does?"

Gina said, "Well, he's been on the social for fifteen months, though he stays up late and sleeps in the day a lot and he goes out evenings and nights. His last job was interior decorating." Gina's face suggested that there was some unusual bit of information about the boy that was awaiting the right question.

"He's got boy-friends?" Momma asked.

"No."

"He's a bloody artist?" This was the Old Man.

Gina shook her head.

"He's enrolled in the Open University and that's why he stays up at night, 'cause they don't have a video," Rosetta, the accountant, offered.

"That's pretty tricky thinking," David said.

Rosetta smiled.

Angelo considered, staring at his wife. "So what's it going to be?" he asked himself aloud. "So what's it going to be?"

"Give up?" Gina asked.

"Never," the Old Man said.

Gina said, "This unemployed layabout kid has a one-year-old

car and a car telephone. And when he goes out at night and his mother asks him what he's been doing, all he will say is, 'Driving.' "

"Well well well," Angelo said. He looked around the table. Everyone else was looking at him. It was a matter of who had driving licences. And who could be asked to stay up all night following the son.

"We could ask Salvatore," Momma said. She didn't like the Old Man to be out at night. There'd been enough of that, one way or another, when he was younger.

Gina said, "Yes. He'd be interested in the work."

"Work?" the Old Man said. "He wants work, he can come here to work, he wants work. Right, Angelo?"

"Sally knows he's always got a place here if he wants it, Poppa," Angelo said. "But he'll never do it."

"Never is a long time," the Old Man said. "But while I'm alive I think I agree with you."

"That'll be forever," Marie said, and the Old Man—who doted on his only granddaughter—beamed and said, "There. Now there's a child."

"I'm glad you like my handiwork, Poppa," Gina said.

The Old Man looked at Gina for a moment and then burst into loud laughter. He also liked his daughter-in-law.

"So how's it left with this woman?" Angelo asked.

"It's left I got the car and its registration number and the address, the car phone number, the names, all that."

"You mean we're on tonight?"

"I already rang Salvatore. He's happy to do the night, or split shifts if you prefer. I didn't know exactly what you had to do tomorrow about the Hardwick."

"Right," Angelo said. "Or we could use Max, or Johnny."

"Outside ops are expensive," Rosetta said.

"Salvatore ain't cheap," Angelo said.

"At least he's in the family," Momma said.

"I'm in the family," the Old Man said. "What's this you treat me like I couldn't follow a giraffe in a herd of mice? Am I not here or something? I got bad breath?"

"I haven't forgotten you, Poppa," Angelo said.

"You're on shoplifting at Quicks again tomorrow," Gina said.

"Cheaper to get a store detective replacement for me daytime than hire an outside op short-notice tonight."

"We're not going to hire anybody tonight except Sal," Angelo said. "I don't know what all this is about. We can cover it. We can cover most things."

"Dad?" David asked.

"Uh-huh?"

"Can I come out with you tonight?"

"I don't know I'm going out."

"Can I go out with Uncle Sal, then?"

"Not on a school night," Gina said.

David said, "I could try to spin you a story about not having school, the teachers having one of those funny days they have or something, but it *is* a school-day tomorrow."

"Is that supposed to be news?" Angelo asked.

"But it's not an important day. No tests and I've got no homework. It's a good day for me to be out the night before."

"Nice try," Angelo said.

"Aw Dad!"

"If we're still on it tomorrow night, maybe then. A Friday or a Saturday night."

"Or both?"

"We'll see. We'll see." Angelo turned back to Gina. "What's the financial?"

"The mother has some money an aunt left her. She intended to fix the house up, but she's too worried about this kid. She's sure he's up to no good."

"What's the name?"

"The boy is John Anson Hatwell."

"Form?"

"I rang Charlie. It's mixed. He had some DC when he was sixteen, for some muggings, and he admitted two burglaries to be taken into account. He's been arrested twice again, for burglaries, but charges were dropped."

"It sounds like a bit of a problem," Angelo said.

"I asked her what she expected if we found out he was engaged in criminal activities. Of course, she wants a chance to 'handle' it herself. I told her that really depended on what we found out, if we found out anything."

"Sal will find out tonight whether the kid is going to be easy to tail or whether we'll need a team."

"So you want Sally on all night? No shifts?"

"Not unless he needs it. If he does then maybe Poppa will cover it." Angelo looked at his father. The Old Man looked at his wife. His wife looked at Gina. "I'll talk to Sally," Gina said, "but we left it that he would do the night unless he heard different."

"So," Angelo said, "you said it was busy. What else came in?"

"Well," Gina said, "there was this woman who found a comb in the back seat of her husband's car. She wanted *him* followed."

"Suddenly it's follow follow follow," Angelo said.

"But she didn't realise how expensive it was or how long it might take."

"To follow a comb?" David asked.

"She went home to think about just how bad she wants to find out who belongs to the comb."

"You should get a grant from the marriage guidance people," Angelo said, "the good advice you give out for free."

"Free free free," David said.

3

At 1055 the next morning Salvatore dropped in to report to Gina on his night's activities.

"The Big Man going to need me again tonight?"

"I don't know yet, Sal," Gina said.

"It's just I got a model booked. I can unbook her if it's important."

"I'll call him on the car phone."

"Or leave a message in his Filofax?"

"Don't be naughty, Salvatore."

Gina tried to ring Angelo, but he wasn't in his car. "Sorry," she said. "I'll try him later."

"I thought it through," Sal said, "and this one, it isn't that important I know ahead. Just let me know around dinnertime, eh?"

"You want to come over for dinner tonight?"

"No thanks, kid." In a playful way he said, "You ever done any modelling?"

"Only in my spare time." An obvious joke, since everyone acknowledged that Gina never had spare time.

"Get hard up, give me a ring."

"You want the money for last night now?"

"Yeah, I'll take it now, now you mention it." He laughed. They both knew who was hard up for what.

Dinner was early on a Friday night to make it easier for David and Marie, who liked to go out. Rosetta went out Fridays too, with her fiancé of the last four years who was agonising over the morality of divorce, if not necessarily over other moralities. Gina always cooked on Fridays, unless it was busy, in which case they went out for a pub meal.

Angelo was already in when Gina came home from the office. He had scrubbed some potatoes.

"So what did Sally have to say?" Angelo asked.

Normally they would have waited to talk about it till mealtime, but with the possibility that David would be riding if Angelo went out, they needed to plan ahead.

"Sally said that John Anson Hatwell didn't have a clue he was being followed and that he should be easy for one car."

"That's something."

"What did he do?"

"Sal got there about 2000. At 2135, Hatwell left his home address alone. He drove into the city and went to a backstreet café called Henry's. Do you know it?"

"That's on Morris Street, isn't it?"

"That's it. Do you know what it is?"

"Give me a clue."

"Stays open all night."

"Cabbies?"

Gina smiled.

Angelo considered the information. "How long was Hatwell there?"

"Only about half an hour. Then drove around till 2 A.M."

"Just drove around?"

"That's what Sally says. He took down the street names for a while, but the kid didn't stop anywhere. He just drove till two-o-eight. He might have been making calls from his car phone, but Sally didn't think so."

"If he did, who to?"

Gina shrugged.

"And what happened then?"

"He picked up a prostitute at two-o-eight."

"I see."

"Dropped her off again at two thirty-two."

"He may have too much money, but he doesn't like to waste it on frills, eh?"

"And then he went home," Gina said.

"Hmmmm."

"His mother says often he stays out till five or six, so this probably wasn't typical. I don't know what he does during the days. It was the evenings and nights that really worried her, and I told her that's what we would concentrate on."

"I think we stick at that for the time being. What she's worried about is how he makes his money, not how he spends it."

Gina nodded.

"I'll take him tonight. Maybe Sally again tomorrow."

"And David?"

They looked at each other. Angelo said, "I more or less promised him."

"Yes," Gina said. "All right."

4

Angelo and David arrived at Hatwell's house at 1830. Their car was well stocked for a long night. Thermos flasks, cassette tapes, food, blankets. Specimen jars in case of emergency. David had been out before and knew the drill.

"Which car is it, Dad?"

"The Opel across the street. Under the light."

"I see."

"How're your eyes these days, son? Can you read the number plate?"

David read the number plate. Then he said, "Grand-dad told Mum that he wanted to come along tonight."

"She didn't say anything to me."

"I think Gran talked him out of it."

"More likely there's a private-eye film on TV. He loves to pick holes in the stories."

"Coincidences like that don't happen in real life," David said, mimicking his grandfather.

Angelo smiled. "That's it."

"Did you ever think of being something other than a private detective, Dad?"

"I didn't get much choice once Uncle Sal went to art college."

"Do you mind?"

"I don't think about it."

"What else would you have wanted to do?"

Angelo considered. "I don't know."

"A painter like Uncle Sal?"

"You got to be able to draw," he said.

"Uncle Sal's stuff doesn't look like you have to draw so well."

"You've got to be able to draw to make it look like you can't," Angelo said.

"Oh," David said. Then, "What time do you think this Hatwell bloke is going to come out of his house?"

"Not for a while yet," Angelo said. "He didn't go out till 2130 last night."

But Angelo was wrong, because three minutes later, at 1922, John Anson Hatwell left his mother's house and got into his car.

"Write it down," Angelo said to David as he started his car.

David took up the clipboard and wrote a note of the time that they had begun the active phase of their surveillance.

5

Hatwell's night began much as the previous night had begun. He drove to Henry's Café, parked and went in.

The windows of the café were large and clear enough that Hatwell could be seen going to the counter, placing an order, and then moving to a table where another man already sat. Hatwell had entered the café at 1949.

The man behind the counter carried a tray to Hatwell at 1953. The man sitting with Hatwell rose and left the café at 1959. This man got into one of the taxis up the street.

"Binoculars," Angelo said with some urgency, but David already had the large-lens binoculars out of the case and resting on the dashboard for support.

When the man pulled his taxi into the road, David read out the vehicle's registration number and the name of the taxi company. Angelo recorded these on the clipboard sheet.

The binoculars intensified light from dim images. It was as if one's eyes were suddenly five times as big: more light from the object was caught.

At 2006 Angelo took some money from his coin purse. "What say you go in and ask for a couple of doughnuts?"

"Really?"

"See whether Hatwell is talking to anybody else, but if he gets up to leave, just walk back to the car."

"Okay, Dad."

"And don't tell your mother."

David winked and put out his hand for the money.

By 2013 he was back in the car. "Hatwell isn't talking to anybody else. What he's got left is some chips on a small plate, and he took a drink from whatever he had a cup of."

Angelo began to speak, but David interrupted him. "There was a mirror behind the counter," he said. "I watched him in that."

"Good boy," he said. Then, "Hang on. I think we're rolling."

Hatwell had risen from his table and was walking towards the café door.

"Got a time for me, Dad?" David asked.

6

Hatwell drove to a petrol station. Angelo pulled into a street on the opposite side of the road, turned around, and waited, ready to go in whichever direction Hatwell chose after his stop.

Hatwell filled his Opel with petrol. David practised with the binoculars and saw that the car had taken 41.42 litres.

"Litres?" Angelo asked. "How much is that in real?"

"A bit more than nine gallons," David said.

"Oh," Angelo said, not having expected an answer. He wrote it down.

Hatwell left the petrol station and drove around for about half an hour. Then, at 2102, he pulled to the side of the road and stopped suddenly. Angelo had to drive past him. David turned to see what was happening in the Opel.

"It looks like he's talking on the phone, Dad," David said.

Angelo again used a side-street and turned around quickly. They could just make out Hatwell's car.

After another minute on the phone, Hatwell put it away and made a squealing U-turn. Angelo pulled out to follow him, and already it was obvious that the car was being driven in a much more positive manner than before.

This went on for thirteen minutes as they followed the Opel

across town. Then suddenly Hatwell slowed down. Taking a
chance, Angelo—who felt he was lucky still to be with the car—
slowed down too, rather than overtake it as he had done the time
before.

Hatwell did not *seem* to notice them.

"If he'd been looking for us," Angelo said to his quiet son,
"he'd have spotted us a dozen times."

Hatwell appeared instead to be intent on finding a house number. After a few moments of slow cruising, he parked. Angelo
pulled past him and parked on the other side of the street.

"Stay here and stay low," he said to David.

Angelo got out of his car. As he pretended to lock the vehicle
door, he saw which way Hatwell had turned. Angelo turned in
the other direction and walked till he found a telephone pole. In
a sideways movement he dropped into its shadow and turned
back to watch Hatwell.

Hatwell had not moved far. For several seconds he studied the
front of a semi-detached house. Then he began to walk. Angelo
followed unseen.

Hatwell walked around the block. When he got to the front of
the semi again, he walked up the path and then through the gate
between the house and its garage.

Angelo slipped back into his car, where David waited eagerly.

"What's up, Dad?"

"I think he's committing a burglary," Angelo said. "If I had
to guess, that would be it." He started his car.

"Where are we going?"

"I want to get in a better position in case he leaves fast."

Angelo turned around in the street and reparked several yards
behind Hatwell's Opel.

They waited for nearly an hour, but eventually Hatwell reap-
peared. He carried two suitcases and was not in any apparent
hurry.

"A cool son of a bitch," Angelo said tensely.

David was pleased that his father used such language with
him. Gina would have disapproved.

Hatwell did not have to unlock his boot. A push of a button

and the lid flew up. In a moment the cases were in and the lid back down. Hatwell got into his car then, and still without seeming to rush, he drove away.

"What do we do now, Dad?"

"Follow follow follow," Angelo said. He pulled out to do just that, but he was in deep thought.

7

Angelo and David came home when Hatwell finally returned to his mother's house, parked, and went in. David, who knew he had been along for something unusual, *said* he was too excited to sleep. But when Angelo sent him upstairs, he went with a yawn, not a murmur. He was too tired to be too excited to sleep.

Angelo left a note on the kitchen table for Gina to wake him at 0800 and to get the Old Man down. On another day Rosetta would have been summoned, but normally she stayed out on a Friday night and did not return on Saturday until noon.

At 0822, when everyone was together and Angelo had had a cup of coffee, he said, "It's tough to know exactly what to do."

He explained what they had done and seen. That Hatwell had pulled up to use his car phone a second time and had driven to look for and find a second address after that. But something had perhaps looked wrong to him. He had not stayed long and had not gone on to the property at the second address.

"And then," Angelo said, "cool as can be, he drives back to Henry's and has some more food. This is at three-twelve in the morning. He's got two suitcases of stolen goods in the boot of his car and he still hasn't locked it because when he finally went back to his mother's house, he locked it before he went inside. We have to decide what to do."

"What does the client want you to do?" the Old Man asked.

Gina said, "She said she wanted to know if there was anything criminal before we told the police."

"How much money have you had?" the Old Man asked.

"Fee for three nights, but no expenses."

"She seem flush?"

"She didn't hesitate writing the cheque," Gina said.

"Our responsibility is to her," the Old Man said.

"I am tempted to follow Hatwell this morning," Angelo said. "To find out what he does with it all. He must be going to take it to a fence today."

"Who's paying you to do that?" the Old Man asked. "Suddenly you're an independent working on commission from the police?"

"I know I know I know, Pop," Angelo said. "All I said was that I am tempted. How often do we get something like this?"

"Not often, but so what?"

"Who paid you to solve the murder of Norman Stiles?"

"At least I was being paid to check a suspect's alibi. So I stumbled on to a different way to alibi him. At least I was being paid."

"You never got paid."

"So at least I was owed," the Old Man said with dignity.

"I know I know I know," Angelo said. "But I am still tempted."

"I think we should contact Mrs. Hatwell," Gina said. "She is the client."

The Old Man looked at Gina fondly.

"I was also tempted to try to look in the boot while Hatwell was in Henry's."

"Not with David there!"

"But Hatwell parked right in front of the café the second time."

They sat quietly for a moment. "We have an obligation to the client," Angelo said. "And an obligation to the police. But if it came to it, I think I could deal with the police."

At the time, they didn't ask him what he meant by that.

Instead, Gina said, "How tired are you?"

"I'm all right."

"This is what we do," Gina said. "We drive two cars to the Hatwells'. I go up to the door to see if I can talk to Mrs. Hatwell myself. You wait outside and you follow the son if he goes anywhere. Poppa mans the office."

"Who's paying, he goes anywhere?" the Old Man demanded again.

"Maybe if we recover what's in the suitcases, the owners will pay us," Gina said.

8

Gina and Angelo arrived at 0949. Before Gina went in, Angelo slipped into her passenger seat. "I'm not that happy about you going in cold," Angelo said.

"I'll be all right."

He raised his eyebrows. "Tell her you're there only as a courtesy. We have to tell the police. We have no choice."

She nodded and got out.

And it was true enough. Police everywhere are territorial. It is not enough that justice be done in the end. If it's their justice, they are loathe for anybody else to administer it. The bulk of a detective agency's business does not require direct involvement in, or knowledge of, illegality; but to be in the bad books of the local police can obstruct detective work a hundred times in a year. It is not something to risk casually.

But Angelo was still tempted to let Hatwell have a little rope and to see where he would take the suitcases.

In the end, however, stronger forces determined his actions.

Gina went to the door of the house at 0954. She was admitted to the house at 0955 by Mrs. Hatwell.

By 1015, Angelo was tired of waiting. He sorely wished he had put a wire on her. Or at least a call device, a button to be pushed in case of emergency. They had relied too much on the assumption that the young Hatwell's routine of sleeping late would be followed. Angelo felt he had been careless from fatigue. He felt that he had put Gina at risk. He began to think that he should go to the house himself.

Having begun to think that, he began to decide to do it.

He got out of his car. He walked towards the house. He stood by the Opel. Gina did not emerge.

Angelo looked at the house. Then he began to walk up the path.

Suddenly the front door burst open. John Anson Hatwell ran out.

Angelo froze. He was in no-man's-land. He couldn't get back to his own car to follow without it being obvious. And Gina still did not appear.

So Angelo tackled Hatwell himself as the young man ran by.

The act was a surprise to both of them. But with Hatwell on the ground, Angelo knew enough to be able to keep him there.

Hatwell swore and spluttered and made enquiries as to what Angelo thought he was doing.

Angelo informed him that he was making a citizen's arrest, something he was perfectly entitled to do as long as he was willing to take the consequences of false citizen's arrest.

Angelo fretted, however, because all he could do was sit there holding Hatwell immobile when what he wanted to do was go into the house to make sure Gina was all right.

Why had Hatwell come out running? What had he done? What had happened to the two women inside. Angelo at first *asked* for answers from Hatwell. Then he screamed at his prisoner.

9

Rosetta served Sunday dinner at 1400 sharp. It was an even-numbered Sunday in the month so her "fiancé," Walter, was in attendance. Salvatore was there too, having brought a model named Carol.

"This is my father," Sal said, introducing her to the Old Man. "And my mother. And this is Carol. She models for me."

"Hello," Momma said tersely. Carol didn't *look* like a potential wife.

"Welcome and make yourself at home," the Old Man said. He shook Carol's hand warmly.

"My niece and nephew, Marie and David."

"Hello."

"Hello."

"Hello."

"Gina you met at the door. That's Rosetta behind the salad bowl and Walter next to her. And the man with the black eye is my brother Angelo. He's about to tell us how he got it."

Carol exchanged greetings with the rest of the family and everyone sat down.

In fact, the one thing that Angelo didn't remember was when he had been hit in the eye. "I was just worried that the creep had done something to my Gina."

Gina said, "The boy's mother was crying. I was trying to console her. She was a client after all."

"But I didn't know."

"No."

"So there I was sitting on this kid," Angelo began, "having made a citizen's arrest."

"Tricky," the Old Man said. "Very tricky."

"I thought I had him bang to rights," Angelo said. "I thought he had two suitcases of stolen goods locked in the boot of his car. I had seen him put them there. I had seen him lock it. I thought—"

"But it was four hours later."

"I know I know I know. Nobody was more surprised than me when the police opened the boot and it was flaming empty."

"That was a very tense moment," Gina agreed.

"I was thinking I'm going to go down for GBH," Angelo said. "A friend, Charlie, may be over there, but he's not going to be able to get me off GBH."

Angelo paused to look around the room.

"So come on," Salvatore said. "Get on with it. How come

you're here and smiling instead of being held on remand in a tin hut somewhere out in the country?"

Gina said, "My Angelo did say before we went out that he thought he could deal with the police."

Angelo said, "I was bothered by this Hatwell's car telephone."

"He didn't use it the night I was out," Sal said.

"But with David and me . . ." Angelo turned to David who beamed at the guests. "With David and me he used it twice. Each time he then goes to a house somewhere. First time it's suitcases. Second time nothing. But it bothered me. And then I'm thinking, each night he's down at this taxi drivers' café. First night he eats alone. Second night he eats with a cabby. You see, the problem about these phone calls is, who is it he's talking to?"

"So my boy puts two and two together," the Old Man said to Carol proudly.

"And he got twenty-two," David said.

"And this time I am lucky," Angelo said.

"Who was it then?" Carol asked.

"What I decided was that Hatwell was working with a taxi driver. The driver picked up fares from a house. He noticed whether they locked up when they left, whether it looked like it was empty. Then after he took them to their destination, he telephoned Hatwell. Gave him the address. Hatwell went to the address, confirmed to his own satisfaction that the house was empty. And burgled it if he thought it was right."

"Gosh," Carol said.

"Some nights the driver got no appropriate fares or maybe he was just off work—that's what I think happened your night, Sal."

Salvatore nodded.

"But Friday night they had a big hit. The police figured there was nearly two grand's worth in the suitcases when they recovered them from the cabby. Who drove home at the end of his shift via Hatwell's house. Duplicate key to Hatwell's boot. Takes the cases at six in the morning. Who sees?"

"They were still in his taxi when the police got there," Gina said.

"And how did you know who the taxi driver was?" Carol asked.

"Ah, that was down to David," Angelo said. "He was the one who spotted the man's registration number when he went on shift. A word with his despatcher and he was despatched."

"All in a night's work, ma'am," David said.

Carol smiled.

"The police say they think it will resolve about forty outstanding burglaries," Gina said.

"Well done, brother," Salvatore said with genuine pride.

"Thanks."

"Are people ready to eat?" Rosetta asked.

"So what's today?" the Old Man asked.

"Linguini, with my special sauce," Rosetta said.

"That's Italian for 'little tongues,' " the Old Man said.

"Oh," Carol said.

"So," the Old Man said to Rosetta, "what's wrong with some curry?"

There was a quiet groan from several places around the table.

"A family joke," Salvatore explained.

"You know, Carol," the Old Man said, "one time, one time only, I was involved in an actual *murder* case."

"Gosh!" Carol said.

"The man's name was Norman Stiles and he was a small-time bookmaker."

A second, louder groan was heard. But not by the Old Man.

Where Is Thy Sting?

Peter Lovesey

The storm had passed, leaving a keen wind that whipped foam off the waves. Heaps of gleaming seaweed were strewn about the beach. Shells, bits of driftwood, and a few stranded jellyfish lay where the tide had deposited them. Paul Molloy, bucket in hand, was down there as he was every morning, alone and preoccupied.

His wife, Gwynneth, stood by the wooden steps that led off the beach through a garden of flowering trees to their property.

"Paul! Breakfast time."

She had to shout it twice more before Paul's damaged brain registered anything. Then he turned and trudged awkwardly towards her.

The stroke last July, a few days before his sixty-first birthday, had turned him into a shambling parody of the fine man he had been. He was left with the physical co-ordination of a small child, except that he was slower. And dumb. The loss of speech was the hardest for Gwynneth to bear. She hated being cut off from his thoughts. He was unable even to write or draw pictures.

She had to be content with scraps of communication. Each time he came up from the beach, he handed her something he had found, a shell or a pebble. She received such gifts as graciously as she had once accepted roses.

They had said at the hospital that she ought to keep talking to him in an adult way, even if he didn't appear to understand. It was a mistake to give up. So she persevered, but inevitably it sounded as if she were addressing a child.

"Darling, what a beautiful shell! Is it for me? Oh, how sweet! I'll take it up to the house and put it on the shelf with all the other treasures you found for me—except that this one must stand in the centre."

She leant forward to kiss him and made no contact with his face. He had moved his head to look at a gull.

She helped him up the steps, and they started the short, laborious trek to the house. They had bought the land, a few miles north of Bundaberg on the Queensland coast, ten years before Paul retired from his Brisbane-based insurance company. As chairman, he could have carried on for years more, but he had always promised he would stop at sixty, before he got fat and feeble, as he used to say. They had built themselves this handsome retirement home and installed facilities they felt they would use: swimming pool, Jacuzzi, boat-house, and tennis court. Only their guests used them now.

"Come on, love, step out quick," she urged Paul. "There's beautiful bacon waiting for you." And tirelessly trying for a spark of interest, she added, "Cousin Haydn's still asleep by the look of it. I don't think he'll be joining your walks on the beach. Not before breakfast, anyway. Probably not at all. Doesn't care for the sea, does he?"

Gwynneth encouraged people to stay. She missed real conversation. Cousin Haydn was on a visit from Wales. He was a distant cousin she hadn't met before, but she didn't mind. She'd got to know him when she'd started delving into her family history for something to distract her. Years ago, her father had given her an old Bible with a family tree in the front. She'd brought it up to date. Then she had joined a family-history society and learnt that a good way of tracking down ancestors was to write to local newspapers in the areas where they had lived. She had managed to get a letter published in a Swansea paper. Haydn had seen it and got in touch. He was an Evans also, and he'd done an immense amount of research. He'd discovered a branch of his family tree that linked up with hers through Great-grandfather Hugh Evans of Port Talbot.

Paul shuffled towards the house without even looking up at the drawn curtains.

"Mind you," Gwynneth continued, "I'm not surprised Haydn is used to staying indoors, what with the Welsh weather I remember. I expect he reads the Bible a lot, being a man of the cloth." She checked herself, for she was speaking the obvious again. She pushed open the kitchen door. "Come on, Paul. Just you and me for breakfast, by the look of it."

Cousin Haydn eventually appeared in time for mid-morning coffee. On the first day after he'd arrived he'd discarded the black suit and dog-collar in favour of a pink T-shirt. Casual clothes made him look several years younger, say forty-five, but they also revealed what Gwynneth would have called a beer-gut had Haydn not been a minister.

"Feel better for your sleep?" she enquired.

"Infinitely better, thank you, Gwynneth." You couldn't mistake him for an Australian when he opened his mouth. "And most agreeably refreshed by a dip in your pool."

"Oh, you had a swim?"

"Hardly a swim. I was speaking of the small circular pool."

She smiled. "The Jacuzzi. Did you find the switch?"

"I was unaware that I needed to find it."

"It works the pumps that make the whirlpool effect. If you didn't switch on, you missed something."

"Then I shall certainly repeat the adventure."

"Paul used to like it. I'm afraid of him slipping now, so he doesn't get in there."

"Pity, if he enjoyed it."

"Perhaps I ought to take the risk. The specialist said he may begin to bring other muscles into use that aren't affected by the stroke. Isn't that so, my darling?"

Paul gave no sign of comprehension.

"Does he understand much?" Haydn asked.

"I convince myself that he does, even if he's unable to show it.

If you don't mind, I don't really care to talk about him in this way, as if he's not one of us."

Cousin Haydn gave an understanding nod. "Let's talk about something less depressing, then. A definite prospect of improvement. I have good news for you, Gwynneth."

She responded with a murmur that didn't convey much enthusiasm. Sermons in church were one thing. Her kitchen was another place altogether.

It emerged that Haydn's good news wasn't of an evangelical character. "One of my reasons for coming here—apart from following up our fascinating correspondence—is to tell you about a mutual ancestor, Sir Tudor Evans."

"Sir Tudor? We had a title in the family?"

"Back in the seventeenth century, yes."

"I don't recall seeing him on my family tree."

Haydn gave the slight smile of one who has a superior grasp of genealogy. "Yours started in the 1780s, if I recall."

"Oh, yes."

"To say that it started then is, of course, misleading. Your eighteenth-century forebears had parents, as did mine, and they, in turn, had parents, and so it goes back, first to Sir Tudor, and ultimately to Adam."

"Never mind Adam. Tell me about Sir Tudor." Gwynneth swung round to Paul, who was sucking his thumb. "Bet you didn't know I came from titled stock, darling."

Haydn said, "A direct line. Planter Evans, they called him. He owned half of Barbados once, according to my research. Made himself a fortune in sugar-cane."

"Really? A fortune. What happened to it?"

"Most of it went down with the *Gloriana* in 1683. One of the great tragedies of the sea. He'd sold the plantations to come back to the land of his fathers. He was almost home when a great storm blew up in the Bristol Channel and the ship was lost with all hands. Sir Tudor and his wife, Eleanor, were among those on board."

"How very sad!"

"God rest their souls, yes."

Gwynneth put her hand to her face. "I'm trying to remember. Last year was such a nightmare for us. A lot of things passed right over my head. The *Gloriana.* Isn't that the ship they found —those treasure-hunters? I read about this somewhere."

"It was in all the papers," Haydn confirmed. "I have some of the cuttings with me, in my briefcase."

"I do remember. The divers were bringing up masses of stuff —coins by the bucketful, silverware and the most exquisite jewellery. Oh, how exciting! Can we make a claim?"

Cousin Haydn shook his head. "Out of the question, my dear. One would need to hire lawyers. Besides, it may be too late."

"Why?"

"As I understand it, when treasure is recovered from a wreck around the British coasts, it has to be handed over to the local receiver of wrecks or the customs. The lawful owner then has a year and a day to make a claim. After that, the pieces are sold and the proceeds go to the salvager."

"A year and a day," said Gwynneth. "Oh, Haydn, this is too tantalising. When did those treasure-hunters start bringing up the stuff?"

"Last March."

"Eleven months! There's still time to make a claim. We must do it."

Haydn sighed heavily. "These things can be extremely costly."

"But we'd get it all back if we could prove our right to the treasure."

He put out his hand in a dissenting gesture. *"Your* right, my dear, not mine. My connection is very tenuous, but yours is undeniable. No, I have no personal interest here. Besides, a man of my calling cannot serve God and Mammon."

"Do you really believe I have a claim?"

"The treasure-hunters would dispute that, I'm sure."

"We're talking about millions of pounds, aren't we? Why should I sit back and let them take it all? I need to get hold of some lawyers—and fast!"

Haydn coughed. "They charge astronomical fees."

"I know," said Gwynneth. "We can afford it, can't we, Paul?"

Paul made a blowing sound with his lips that probably had no bearing on the matter.

Gwynneth assumed so. "What is it they want—a down payment?"

"A retainer, I think, is the expression."

"I can write a cheque tomorrow, if you want. I look after all our personal finances now. There's more than enough in the deposit account. The thing is, how do I find a reliable lawyer?"

Haydn cupped his chin in his hands and looked thoughtful. "I wouldn't go to an Australian firm. Better find someone on the spot. Jones. Heap and Jones of Cardiff are the best in Wales. I'm sure they could take on something like this."

"But is there time? We're almost into March now."

"It is rather urgent," Haydn agreed. "Look, I don't mind cutting my holiday short by a few days. If I got back to Wales at the weekend, I could see them on Monday."

"I couldn't ask you to do that," said Gwynneth in a tone that betrayed the opposite.

"No trouble," said Haydn breezily.

"You're an angel. Would they accept a cheque in Australian dollars?"

"That might be difficult, but it's easily got around. Travellers' cheques are the thing. I use them all the time. In fact, if you're serious about this . . ."

"Oh, yes."

". . . you could buy sterling travellers' cheques in my name and I could pay the retainer for you."

"Would you really do that for me?"

"Anything to be of service."

She shivered with pleasure. "And now, if you've got them nearby, I'd love to have ten minutes with those press cuttings."

He left them with her, and she read them through several times during the afternoon when she was alone in her room and Paul had gone for one of his walks along the beach. Three pages cut from a colour supplement had stunning pictures of the finds. She so adored the ruby necklace and the gold bracelets that she thought she would refuse to sell them. Cousin Haydn had also given her a much more detailed family tree than she had seen before. It proved beyond doubt that she was the only direct descendant of Sir Tudor Evans.

Was it all too good to be true?

One or two doubts crept into her mind later that afternoon. Presumably the treasure-hunters had invested heavily in ships, divers, and equipment. They must have been confident that anything they brought up would belong to them. Maybe her claim wasn't valid under the law. She wondered also whether Cousin Haydn's research was entirely accurate. She didn't question his good faith—how could one in the circumstances?—but she knew from her own humble diggings in family history that it was all too easy to confuse one Evans with another.

On the other hand, she told herself, that's what I'm hiring the lawyers to find out. It's their business to establish whether my claim is lawful.

There was an unsettling incident towards evening. She walked down to the beach to collect Paul. The stretch where he liked to wander was never particularly crowded, even at weekends, and she soon spotted him kneeling on the sand. This time he didn't need calling. He got up, collected his bucket, and tottered towards her.

Automatically, she held out her hand for the gift he had chosen for her. He peered into the bucket and picked something out and placed it on her open palm.

A dead wasp.

She almost snatched her hand away and let the thing drop. She was glad she didn't, because it was obvious that he'd saved it for her and she would have hated to hurt his feelings.

She said, "Oh, a little wasp. Thank you, darling. So thoughtful. We'll take it home and put it with all my pretty pebbles and shells, shall we?"

She took a paper tissue from her pocket and folded the tiny corpse carefully between the layers. In the house she unwrapped it and made a space on the shelf among the shells and stones.

"There." She turned and smiled at Paul.

He put his thumb on the wasp and squashed it.

"Darling!"

The small act of violence shocked Gwynneth. She found herself quite stupidly reacting as if something precious had been destroyed. "You shouldn't have done that, Paul! You gave it to me. I treasure whatever you give me. You know that."

He shuffled out of the room.

That evening over the meal, she told Cousin Haydn about the incident, once again breaking her own rule and discussing Paul while he was sitting with them. "I keep wondering if he meant anything by it," she said. "It's so unlike him."

"If you want my opinion," said Haydn, "he showed some intelligence. You don't want a wasp in the house, dead or alive. As a matter of fact, I've got quite a phobia about them. It's one of the reasons why I avoid the beach. You can't sit for long on any beach without being troubled by them."

"Perhaps you were stung once?"

"No, I've managed to avoid them, but one of my uncles was killed by one."

"Killed by a wasp?"

"He was only forty-four at the time. It happened on the front at Aberystwyth. He was stung here, on the right temple. His face went bright red and he fell down on the shingle. My aunt ran for a doctor, but all he could do was confirm that uncle was dead."

Clearly the tragedy had made a profound impression on Haydn. His account of the incident, spoken in simple language instead of his usual florid style, carried conviction.

"Dreadful. It must have been a rare case."

"Not so uncommon as you'd think. I tell you, Gwynneth, the wasp is one of God's creatures I studiously avoid at all times." He turned to Paul and for the first time addressed him directly, trying to end on a less grave note. "So I say more power to your thumb, boyo."

Paul looked at him blankly.

Towards the end of the meal Haydn announced that he would be leaving in the morning. "I telephoned the airport. I am advised I can get something called a stand-by. They say it's better before the weekend, so I'm leaving tomorrow."

"*Tomorrow?*" said Gwynneth, her voice pitched high in alarm. "But you can't. We haven't bought those travellers' cheques."

"That's all right, my dear. There's a place to purchase them at the airport. All you need to do is write me a cheque. In fact, you could write it now in case we forget in the morning."

"How much?"

"I don't know. I'm not too conversant with the scale of fees lawyers charge these days. Are you sure you want to get involved in expense?"

"Absolutely. If I have no right to make a claim, they'll let me know, won't they?"

"I'll let you know myself, my dear. How much can you spare without running up an overdraft? It's probably better for me to take more, rather than less."

She wrote him a cheque for ten thousand Australian dollars.

"Then if you will excuse me, I shall go and pack my things and have a quiet hour before bedtime."

"Would you like an early breakfast tomorrow?"

He smiled. "Early by my standards, yes. Say about eight? That gives me ample time to do something I promised—try the Jacuzzi with the switch on. Goodnight and God bless you, my dear. And you, Paul, old fellow."

Gwynneth slept fitfully. At one stage in the night she noticed that Paul had his eyes open. She found his hand and gripped it tightly and talked to him as if he understood. "I keep wondering if I've done the right thing, giving Haydn that cheque. It's not as if I don't trust him—I mean, you've got to trust a man of God, haven't you? I just wonder if you would have done what I did, my darling, giving him the cheque, I mean, and somehow I don't think so. In fact, I ask myself if you were trying to tell me something when you gave me the wasp. It was such an unusual thing for you to do. Then squashing it like that."

She must have drifted off soon after because when she next opened her eyes the grey light of dawn was picking out the edges of the curtains. She sighed and turned towards Paul, but his side of the bed was empty. He must have gone down to the beach already.

She showered and dressed soon after, wanting to make an early start on cooking the breakfast. She would get everything ready first, she decided, and then fetch Paul from the beach before she started the cooking. However, this was a morning of surprises.

For some unfathomable reason Paul had already come up from the beach without being called. He was seated in his usual place in the kitchen.

"Paul! You gave me quite a shock," Gwynneth told him. "What is it? Are you extra hungry this morning or something? I'll get this started presently. Would you like some bread while you're waiting? Better give Cousin Haydn a call first and make sure he's awake."

It crossed her mind as she went to tap on Haydn's door that Paul hadn't brought her anything from the beach. She wondered if she'd hurt his feelings by talking about the wasp as she had.

She didn't like knocking on Haydn's door in case she was interrupting his morning prayers, but it had to be done this morning in case he overslept.

He answered her call. "Thank you. Is there time for me to sample the Jacuzzi?"

"Of course. Shall we say twenty minutes?"

"That should be ample."

She returned to the kitchen and made a sandwich for Paul. The bucket he always took to the beach was beside him. Without being too obvious about it, Gwynneth glanced inside to see if the customary gift of a shell or a pebble was there. It was silly, but she was feeling quite neglected.

Empty.

She said nothing about it. Simply busied herself setting the table for breakfast. Presently she started heating the frying pan.

Fifteen minutes later when everything was cooked and waiting in the oven, Haydn had not appeared.

"He's really enjoying that Jacuzzi," she told Paul. "We'd better start, I think."

They finished.

"I'd better go and see," she said.

When she went to the door, the leg of Paul's chair was jammed against it, preventing her from opening it. "Do you mind, darling? I can't get out."

He made no move.

"Maybe you're right," Gwynneth said, always willing to assume that Paul's behaviour was deliberate and intelligent. "I shouldn't fuss. It won't spoil for being left a few minutes more."

She allowed another quarter of an hour to pass. "Do you think something's happened to him? I'd better go and see, really I had. Come on, dear. Let me through."

As she took Paul by the arm and helped him to his feet he reached out and drew her towards him, pressing his face against hers. She was surprised and delighted. He hadn't embraced her once since the stroke. She turned her face and kissed him before going to find Cousin Haydn.

Haydn was lying face down on the tile surround of the Jacuzzi, which was churning noisily. He was wearing black swimming-trunks. He didn't move when she spoke his name.

"I think he may be dead," she told the girl who took the emergency call.

The girl told her to try the kiss of life. An ambulance was on its way.

Gwynneth was still on her knees trying to breathe life into Cousin Haydn when the police arrived. They had come straight round the back of the house.

"Let's have a look, lady." After a moment the sergeant said, "He's gone—no question. Who is he—your husband?"

She explained about Cousin Haydn.

"This is where you found him?"

"Well, yes. Was it an electric shock, do you think?"

"You tell me, lady. Was the Jacuzzi on when you found him?"

"Yes." Gwynneth suddenly realised that it was no longer running. Paul must have switched it off while she was phoning for help. She didn't want Paul brought into this. "I don't know. I may be mistaken about that."

"You see, there could be a fault," the sergeant speculated. "We'll get it checked. Is your husband about?"

"He was." She called Paul's name. "He must have gone down to the beach. That's where he goes." She told them about the stroke.

More policemen arrived, some in plain clothes. One introduced himself as Detective Inspector Perry. He talked to Gwynneth several times in the next two hours. He went into Cousin Haydn's room and opened the suitcase he had packed for the flight home.

"You say you knew this man as Haydn Evans, your cousin from Wales?"

"That's who he was."

"A distant cousin?"

Gwynneth didn't care for his grin. "I can show you the family tree if you like."

"No need for that, Mrs. Molloy. His luggage is stuffed with family trees, all as bogus as his Welsh accent. He wasn't a minister of any church or chapel. His name was Brown. Michael Herbert Brown. An English con-man we've been after for months. He was getting too well known to Scotland Yard, so he came out to Queensland this summer. Been stinging people for thousands with the treasure-hunting story. Here's your cheque. Lucky escape, I'd say."

They finally took the body away in an ambulance.

Detective Inspector Perry phoned late in the afternoon. "Just thought I'd let you know that your Jacuzzi is safe to use, Mrs. Molloy. There's no electrical fault. I have the pathologist's report and I can tell you that Brown was not electrocuted."

"What killed him, then?"

He laughed. "Sort of appropriate. It was a sting."

Gwynneth frowned and put her hand to her throat as she recalled what Cousin Haydn had told her. "A sting from a wasp?"

"In a manner of speaking." There was amusement in his voice. "Not the wasp you had in mind."

"I don't understand."

"No mystery in it, Mrs. Molloy. A sea wasp got him. You know what a sea wasp is?"

She knew. Everyone on the coast knew. "A jellyfish. An extremely poisonous jellyfish."

"Right, a killer."

"But Haydn didn't swim in the sea. He kept off the beach."

"That explains it, then."

"How?"

"He wouldn't have known about the sea wasps. That storm washed quite a number on to the beaches. Looks as if Brown decided to take one look at the sea before he left this morning. He'd put on his swimming gear—we know that—and he must have waded in. Didn't need to go far. There were sea wasps stranded in the shallows. You and I know how deadly they are, but I reckon an Englishman wouldn't. He got bitten, staggered back to the house, and collapsed beside the Jacuzzi."

"I see." She knew it was nonsense.

"Try and remember, Mrs. Molloy. Did you see him walk down to the beach?"

"I was cooking breakfast."

"Pity. Where was your husband?"

"Paul?" She glanced over at Paul, now sitting in his usual armchair with his arms around his bucket. "He was with me in the kitchen." She was about to add that Paul had come up from the beach, but the inspector was already on to other possibilities.

"Maybe someone else saw Brown on the beach. I believe it's pretty deserted at that time?"

"Yes."

"Be useful to have a witness for the inquest. All right, I heard what you said about him normally keeping off the beach, but it's a fact that he died from a seawasp sting. That's been established."

"I'm not questioning it."

"I ask you, Mrs. Molloy, how else could it have happened? There's only one other possibility I can think of. How could a jellyfish get into a Jacuzzi, for Christ's sake?"

A Fine Art

Jill McGown

Gerald got off the bus and stepped out into the sultry morning. He waited for a lull in the Monday traffic which streamed past, and took deep breaths of air already heavy with exhaust fumes. Perhaps he gripped the briefcase too tightly as he crossed the road to the station, but he looked just like everyone else. Just like any other successful young City gent. And until Friday evening, that was just what he had been. Until Friday evening.

"Surely you're not doing that *now?*" asked Paula. "You'll be late for your concert."

"Of course I won't," said Gerald, as he began to piece the light fitting together again. The early evening news was just starting; he wouldn't have begun the job if he hadn't had time to complete it. "It had to be done," he said, stepping off the stool, and going over to the switch. "So it might as well be done straight away." The light came on, and he smiled at Paula. "Never put off . . ." he said.

"Please don't start quoting maxims, Gerald."

There was a silence after she had spoken, broken by the TV newsreader, who said that there were fears of terrorist activity in the capital over the weekend.

"I wasn't aware that quoting maxims was something I was given to doing," he said.

"And don't be so pompous!"

Pompous? For a moment, he felt a little hurt. But she wasn't feeling well, of course. That would explain it. Though she had seemed a little cool lately. Ever since the party, really. He frowned. Perhaps she hadn't been well for some time, and hadn't wanted to worry him with it.

"Maybe I shouldn't go," he said.

"Oh no. I don't want to spoil your evening too," she said. "You go. You've been looking forward to it for ages."

She didn't look too bad, he thought. In fact, she looked her usual, healthy, pretty self. It was probably just the thundery weather, as she had said. He smiled again. "If you're sure," he said. "I'll go and change."

No one joined him at his table for two as he dined alone, permitting himself a small sherry beforehand. But a last-minute concert-goer had his optimism rewarded by getting Paula's seat, and Gerald felt vaguely contemptuous of him as he settled himself down. Totally disorganised. Coming on spec to a concert like this. Gerald shifted a little in his seat, crossing his legs away from his neighbour, in unconscious rejection of this lack of discipline incarnate.

The orchestra and the audience waited for the conductor, but he didn't arrive. Instead, the sober-faced manager walked on to the podium; there was a smattering of applause from people who didn't know any better.

Groans greeted the announcement that the evening's programme had had to be cancelled because of a bomb threat; there was much scepticism and no panic as they filed out obediently. Gerald felt the pang of guilt that he always felt when his countrymen were active on the mainland. Guilt that his compatriots blew people up? Or guilt that he had opted out of the unpleasantness altogether? He wasn't sure. But he didn't like it when he couldn't place the Irish Sea firmly between him and them. Not that he would ever have become involved, even if he had stayed; his mother had always hurried him past the tough little boys with the toy guns, who played at soldiers. He had followed her example as he grew up, and perhaps, he thought, that was where this odd sense of guilt sprang from. It had been a hoax, anyway, according to the car radio.

Dusk was falling as he arrived home. Downstairs was in darkness, but a light was on in the bedroom. Gerald cut the engine and coasted down the incline. He didn't put the car away, because the garage door made such a whine, and he didn't want to waken her if she had managed to get to sleep. Worriedly, he dug in his pocket for his door key. It wasn't like Paula to go to bed early, even when she was one degree under. She was a night-owl, and he had long ago given up trying to reform her. He usually went up a full two hours before she did; he had to have a decent night's sleep. So she must feel really bad if she had gone to bed. He opened the door carefully, silently, and closed it without letting it so much as click.

His foot was on the bottom tread when he heard what sounded like a moan. But even in the instant that he took to gather himself to run up to her, he heard a corresponding, unmistakably masculine grunt, and he froze. His foot on the stair, his hand on the banister, poised ready to run to his wife's sick bed, he listened in paralysed horror as the sounds increased in intensity. When he at last moved, it was to cover his ears. Then, slowly, he took his hands away and left the house as silently as he had entered.

He sat in the car and looked up at the lit bedroom window. Who was he? Where did she meet him? Why, *why?* Would she go off with him, whoever he was? Was he going to lose her? He couldn't, he couldn't lose her. It had never occurred to him to consider the possibility before. But whoever that was up there was going to take her from him; she was having an affair with someone else, had fallen in love with someone else.

He got out of the car, easing the door shut, and stood in the shadow of the garage. Eventually, the hall light went on, and he emerged, a slight figure in dark clothes. Gerald frowned, momentarily unable to place the thin, handsome face. Paula didn't come out with him, and he closed the front door, standing irresolutely for a moment, looking at Gerald's car.

John Sheldon, of course. Sheldon, who lived his life with all the arrogance that his inherited wealth allowed. A friend of the famous and infamous, who boasted of his connections with the

underworld, of his spell in prison for possession of marijuana, of
the driving ban that he'd just completed, of the women that he'd
had. But Paula? Paula had been distant, polite, when they'd met
him. A mutual friend had invited them to one of Sheldon's par-
ties, where every other face was well known; Gerald and Paula
had left when their overgrown schoolboy of a host had produced
the cocaine. Paula had found him just as appalling as he had.

The evidence argued against that. And Gerald was forced to
concede that the man did have a kind of superficial attraction.
The attraction of the rebel, he supposed. Gerald came from a
background where it was almost rebellious simply to conform.
But there was nothing glamorous about observing speed limits
and working a ten-, often twelve-hour day. It had produced the
trappings of wealth in Gerald's case, but no time to enjoy them.

Sheldon turned back towards the house, then shrugged
slightly, turned again, and walked away. Gerald watched his
retreating figure, and he could see how it had happened. Sheldon
had never come across a woman who hadn't fallen at his feet, so
he'd made it his business to see that Paula was no exception.
He'd seduced her with glitz and glamour, and made her see how
boring and uneventful her life with Gerald was. A rebel who
cocked a snook at authority—he could see that Paula could be
attracted by that. Easy enough to be a rebel if you didn't have to
work. But Paula had fallen for it, fallen for *him.* And what could
he do against someone like Sheldon? Someone who had had
everything Gerald worked so hard for handed to him on a plate
and didn't have to conform to anyone's rules? What if she went
away with him? His hands went to his ears again, as though he
could block out the memory of what he had overheard.

He was reversing the car out of the driveway, driving off after
Sheldon. He didn't know what he was going to do—talk to him,
plead with him. Anything. He had to stop him stealing Paula
from him. The car nosed its way down the narrow street to the
building site, alongside which Sheldon was walking. There was
no point in appealing to the man's sense of honour, because he
didn't have one. He had broken up other marriages; he would

take Paula away from him, and Paula was why Gerald lived. He couldn't bear to lose her.

He could see Sheldon's car, parked on the opposite side of the road from the building site. And Sheldon, sauntering along, stepping off the pavement. He hated him for existing; Gerald's foot went down on the accelerator, and a sudden, breathtaking surge of power pumped through his whole body as the car went straight and true for Sheldon.

He scrambled out and ran back to his victim, kneeling down, feeling for signs of life. There were none. It had been swift and efficient. And he had made certain that Sheldon could never take Paula away, God forgive him. Gerald crossed himself. And God bless the money-grubbing property developers who knocked down the mean little houses and built homes fit for yuppies. For no one had seen, no one had heard.

He walked back to the car, sizing up the boot. Just about. Sheldon presented little difficulty to Gerald, even as a dead weight, and he hoisted the body on to his shoulder and tipped it into the boot like a sack of the cement that had made Sheldon senior's original profits. Sheldon's keys lay in the road, and Gerald stooped to pick them up. He had to go to Sheldon's place; he had to make sure that there was nothing of Paula's there. Nothing to connect him to Sheldon. Then, he'd sort out what to do with the body.

He should be feeling frightened, he told himself. He was driving along with a man's body in the boot of his car. But he felt exhilarated, almost jubilant, as he at last arrived at the quiet private mews where Sheldon lived. On a Friday evening, only one or two incurious lights glowed in the windows, and no one saw him let himself in with Sheldon's key.

As he searched the rooms, he was only barely aware of the car, *his* car, parked outside with a body in its boot. He was still on a high from the power-surge. And he found nothing. No sign, no trace of Paula's presence. He began to think of his next move. Dump the body? Or just report the car stolen? Leave it there, complete with body, and report it stolen. Yes. Yes, he'd probably do that. He opened the door to leave and found himself face to face with two men. His heart stopped beating.

"Vinny sent us," said the first, a small man with wiry hair.

"Who are you?" Gerald heard himself saying.

"Never mind names."

Gerald swallowed.

"He said to make sure you wasn't stoned," said the other.

Gerald's eyes widened slightly. They thought he was Sheldon.

"He said we had to give you your instructions," said the first.

"You . . . you'd better come in." Gerald stood aside.

"He looks a bit windy to me," observed the second man, a tall, gaunt figure in black. "Will he be OK?"

"Vinny says he's OK."

It irritated Gerald, even under these bizarre circumstances, to be talked about as though he wasn't there.

"Is that your car outside?" asked the tall one.

"Yes." There seemed little point in lying, whoever they were.

"Where's the other one?" asked the small man.

"What?"

"You were supposed to be getting a car. Where is it?"

Gerald's working life was spent thinking quickly, acting quickly. And bluffing.

"You don't need to know where it is," he said calmly.

The small man nodded, and a glimmer of something like respect came into his eye. And then he began, as promised, to give Gerald his instructions. Sheldon's instructions.

My God, they were going to rob a bank. Not an ordinary bank. One which only existed to provide safety-deposit boxes for its customers. And Vinny, it seemed, had spent a great deal of money working out how to break into it without anyone being any the wiser until the bank opened again on Monday. Sheldon's job didn't sound too arduous. He had to keep lookout, tell them if it was safe to come up, open the boot, and be ready to drive off once the others were in the car. If there was trouble, he would have to outdrive the police, but there would be no trouble. Sheldon was to meet the small man at seven o'clock on Saturday morning, and he would take him to the tunnel exit. It was a long way away from the bank, away from anywhere. Sheldon would be home in time for lunch. Sweet as a nut it would be.

The small man gestured to the door, and they seemed to be leaving. Outside, the thin one ran a hand over Gerald's car. "Nice motor," he said.

Gerald stiffened slightly. Go on, he thought. Get your fingerprints on it. Then they'll believe me that it was stolen. He reached into his pocket, and took out his own keys. "Here," he said; holding them out. "Have a drive, if you like."

"Can I?"

"No!" barked the small man. "If you're seen riding around in one of them . . ."

The other took Gerald's keys. "Just a look," he assured his companion. Gerald watched, tense, as he opened the door, sat in the car, touched the steering wheel, the dash, everything.

"I'm for one of these," he said. "When we've done." He put the keys in the ignition.

"Out," said the boss, and reluctantly the other man eased his tall frame out of the car.

"Just leave the keys," Gerald said, striving to sound unconcerned. "I'm going out."

And there it was, after they'd gone. Covered with fingerprints almost certainly known to the police. Covered with someone *else's* fingerprints at any rate. Gerald felt cock-a-hoop as he left Sheldon's place, walking a long, safe distance before hailing a taxi.

"Did you enjoy the concert?" Paula asked.

"It was cancelled," he said. "Bomb scare."

He had gone for a drive, he explained, intending to go back to the hall in case they had given the all-clear for the concert to start after all. But the car had packed up on him, and it took forever to get a taxi.

"I thought I heard your car earlier," she said.

"No. Must have been someone turning in the road."

It was perfect. Perfect. God was on his side.

But the supercharge didn't last forever, and as he lay in bed, his belief in God's partisanship waned with it. It was still his car. It had still killed someone, someone who was still in the boot. Someone known to Gerald. Vinny, he had been told, would have Sheldon's legs broken if he fouled up this job. But murder? And anyway, if the job didn't take place, then the police could hardly connect Sheldon's death to it, could they? So what would make Vinny move on to murder from grievous bodily harm? Being double-crossed, Gerald supposed. If the job *did* take place, and Sheldon . . .

Gerald sat up, sweating in the oppressive, thundery heat. Suppose Sheldon did turn up? Turned up, but then robbed them of the loot? Then Vinny could well get murderous. And there would be a moment. Just a single moment, when the haul would be in the boot, and the others not yet in the car. If he could just put his foot down again. Like he had with Sheldon. But he needed a car. A car, a car—Sheldon's car, of course. Parked across from the building site, powerful as his own. Gerald remembered the sensation of all that power transferring itself from the engine to him, and he wanted to feel it again.

He wore a business suit, because he would be carrying a briefcase, and he mustn't look odd. He wore driving gloves. And he had a plan, a plan that would put all these crooks behind bars where they belonged, and leave him in the clear.

It took longer than they thought, and it was well after lunchtime when Gerald finally heard the tapped signal. There was no one around; there had been no one all morning, in this unlovely, unproductive, uninhabited cul-de-sac. Gerald dragged away the manhole cover and opened the boot, as instructed. He watched, revving the engine nervously, as the small man emerged and the sack was handed up to him by the other. The tall man was pushing back the manhole cover, the other dropped the sack in the boot.

Again, the growling power of the engine charged into Gerald's body as he roared away, the boot still open. His only regret was that he couldn't see them in the mirror as he disappeared from their view. He stopped, slammed down the boot with his gloved hand, and drove off again, this time within the speed limit. And it was difficult, keeping to the snail's pace laid down, when he knew that he had all that potency inside him. But he drove like the model driver he was, back to the building site. Back to where he had rid himself of the threat to his security. They were working on the site, taking no notice of him as he opened the boot. They didn't know that he was emptying jewellery and cash from a sack to a briefcase. All of it, except one particularly beautiful diamond ring. For that was going to be in Sheldon's pocket when they found him. Along with the key to a left-luggage locker.

Gerald walked home, unremarkable in his pin-striped suit, carrying his briefcase. He had to wait until tomorrow to carry on with his plan. Tomorrow, when he would know for certain that the bank really was unaware that a robbery had taken place, and it would be safe for him to use Sheldon's car again. And safe to plant the ring on Sheldon. Right now, Vinny's boys would be there, tearing the place apart. When they found nothing, they'd go looking for Sheldon. And if they looked in the boot of the car, what they would find there would scare them off for good.

He went straight upstairs and hid the briefcase in the spare room. He felt good; it was only when he walked into the living room and saw Paula reading, curled up in an armchair, that the power suddenly drained away, and he began to shake uncontrollably.

A drink. A drink would steady him. He walked almost blindly to the sideboard, and half filled a tumbler with whisky, drinking it down like lemonade. It hurt; it knocked his breath away.

"Gerald?" Paula twisted round. "Gerald, for God's sake! What's wrong?"

"Nothing," he croaked. He poured another as he spoke, the bottle rattling against the glass. He had to stop the shaking, drown the terrible dread in the pit of his stomach. How long did it take to work? *Did* it work? He'd never tried it before.

"Gerald, what are you doing? Where have you been?"

"To the car," he said, the lines that he had rehearsed surfacing through the fog of panic. "It's been stolen."

"I thought it wouldn't go," she said.

"It obviously went for them," said Gerald. He drained his glass again, the liquor burning his throat, and poured another, bringing the bottle with him as he sat down.

"Gerald, what are you *doing?*" she asked again. She looked at the bottle at his feet, her face bewildered. "What did the police say?"

"I haven't told them yet," he said, desperately trying to stop his hand shaking as he lifted the glass to his lips.

"Gerald—it's just a car. It's insured." She frowned. "Was there something in it?" she asked. "Something important?"

There was something in it, all right, he thought. But he was prepared for that question too, and he told her what he would tell the police when they asked. "Just my briefcase," he said, gulping down half of what was in the glass. Come on, come on. Work.

"Gerald—you can't drink whisky like that! You'll make yourself ill!"

No. It would make him better. At last there was a numbing sensation round his mouth. It was working, and it wasn't burning his throat any more. It was going down smoothly and sweetly, like fresh water.

"Gerald, stop that!" She scrambled to her feet. "You can kill yourself doing that!" She came over to him and took away his empty glass, picking up the bottle. She looked at it, then at him. "Oh God!" she said. "This isn't about the car, is it?"

His head was beginning to feel a bit muzzy, and that line hadn't been in the script that he'd rehearsed all morning.

"It *was* you I heard last night, wasn't it?" she said. "You did come home. When the concert was cancelled. You came home, didn't you?"

He looked up at her. She was beautiful. Really, really beautiful. No wonder Sheldon had wanted to add her to his collection. And he didn't blame her for falling for Sheldon. Sheldon had

seduced her. He was glamorous, exciting. He lived on the edge
of disaster all the time. And it ought to be distasteful, but it
wasn't. It was exciting. Exciting to feel the rush of adrenalin,
even exciting not to know how long it would last. Oh, Paula
should have seen him when he drove off, leaving Vinny's stooges
standing.

"That's all it was," she was saying. "I'm sorry. But that's
what happened, and I can't change it. I wish to God I could."

He had been aware that she had been speaking; he had heard
her voice, the rise and fall. No words. He couldn't understand
the words. He couldn't see her properly. He felt very strange. "I
love you, Paula," he said, his voice thick and hoarse. "I don't
blame you." His head swam.

"No. No, Gerald. Get up. Get up—you can't pass out. Gerald, get *up!*"

She was pulling at him, putting her arms round him, pulling
him off the sofa. She couldn't lift a big man like him, he thought.
He'd have to help. And he staggered to his feet, leaning on her,
as she slid open the door, taking him out onto the patio, telling
him to breathe fresh air, walking him up and down in the tiny
space. In a moment of clarity, he knew what was going to happen and broke away from her just before he was violently and
painfully sick.

She must have put him to bed. He couldn't remember. He
hadn't known that it was possible to have so much pain in your
head. He still felt sick. And he had things to do . . . He stumbled as he got up, shakily righting himself. It was morning.
What time was it? Only ten o'clock. It was all right. If he lived,
he'd got plenty of time. If he died, then none of it mattered.

The pain had gone by the time he heard Paula's key in the
door. He felt hollow and weak, and the smell and taste of the
whisky still clung to him through a bath and several brushings of
his teeth. Paula didn't speak; she made coffee and brought it to
him, sitting beside him on the sofa.

"Are you better?" she asked softly.

He nodded. "Where have you been?" he asked.

"Mass."

Paula hadn't been to church for years. That was another thing
he'd nagged her about.

"Good for the soul and all that," she said, almost in tears. "I
explained to Father Gallagher that you weren't well." She took
his hands in hers. "I'm so sorry, Gerald."

"He wouldn't have made a fool of himself," Gerald said. "He
wouldn't have thrown up on the patio."

"Father Gallagher?" she asked, startled.

"Sheldon!"

"Oh." She gave a short sigh. "I imagine he has, in his time,"
she said.

"Paula," he said. "I understand, you know. I understand why
you had an affair with him. But . . ." He looked at her. "I can't
live like he does. I have to—"

"Gerald," she said, interrupting him. "I told you yesterday.
John Sheldon doesn't mean a thing to me."

"What?" He stared at her, bemused.

"Please believe me, Gerald. I know why I did it. I was angry
with you. Because you . . . you're so straight. So rigid. You
made me leave the party, and I didn't *want* to leave."

His eyes widened. "You wanted to stuff cocaine up your
nose?"

"No! But I didn't want to leave just because other people were
going to. I felt . . . I felt humiliated, Gerald. It was ridiculous
and childish, I know. But I was angry, and that's why I rang
him up. That's why it happened. There was nothing more to it
than that."

"What?" he said again, his mouth dry.

"Please believe me. It wasn't an affair, Gerald. It was a one-
night stand. I felt that I had something to prove, I suppose. But
it didn't mean a thing, I swear."

His mouth hung open as he looked at her. "But . . ." he
began, wanting to tell her what he had done. Tell her that Sheldon was dead. Because of her. Dead in the boot of his car. But
he couldn't tell her that he was a murderer. So he told her what

she was, instead. Using words that he had never uttered before. Words that once he wouldn't have tolerated being spoken in her presence. And when he had run out of names to call her, he stood up. "I'm going," he said, his back to her. He couldn't look at her.

"All right." She sounded hurt and angry and frightened. "If that's what you think of me, maybe you should go." Her voice shook. "But I love you, Gerald. And I wish you could forgive me."

"I do," he said, still not looking at her. "I have." He sighed. "I have things to do."

"Can't they wait?"

"What for?"

She touched his shoulder, and he turned to her. He had something to prove too. To himself, to Paula. Now. Now, while he could still remember the tremendous sensation of power surging through him, as he killed for her. *Killed* for her. Boring, straight, staid old Gerald would prove that Sheldon wasn't the only one who could excite her. Now. Everything else could wait. He'd go afterwards.

He woke to darkness, alone in the bed, and fumbled for the clock. The glowing digits told him it was half past nine, and he lay back, telling himself that he must get up. He must go and put the finishing touches to this whole ghastly business. But he didn't move.

Because all that their brief, unsatisfactory union had proved was that even his normal reserves of energy were exhausted. He had fallen into a defeated sleep, with Paula assuring him that it didn't matter, while the sounds of Sheldon's successful trespass echoed in his memory, mocking him. It mattered. It *mattered.*

He was tired. He didn't want to go out. His limbs ached, and he just wanted to stay there, alone in the darkness. If he went early enough in the morning, he could still beat the bank to it. It would take time to discover the robbery, time to call the police, time to alert everyone.

Yes, he thought. Monday morning. That would be even better. No one would look twice at him leaving something in a left-luggage locker, putting something in the boot of a car. He couldn't use Sheldon's car, though. It would be too risky tomorrow. But he could get the bus. His car had been stolen, hadn't it? What more natural? Yes, he thought, closing weary eyes again. Tomorrow would be time enough.

Gerald woke again at ten past five, when a peal of distant thunder disturbed the air. He gently eased himself out of bed so as not to disturb the sleeping Paula and prepared to complete his plan.

Gerald stepped on to the pavement and could see a news-agent's billboard for the evening paper on the streets already. Something big must have happened, and Gerald's heart pumped as he drew closer to it. Not the robbery. Please God, not the robbery.

BOMB BLAST AT VICTORIA—TWO DEAD, it read.

The thunder that had wakened him had not been thunder; it had been a bomb which had claimed lives. There was no guilt. Perhaps it never had been guilt. All that the bomb meant to him was that the robbery would be playing second fiddle to it as far as the police were concerned.

And now, all he had to do was walk into the station, leave the briefcase, then come out again, joining the commuters as they made their way to the tubes. On to Sheldon's place, where he would open the boot of his car, plant the ring and the key, go to work as normal, and report his car missing. The confidence was back in Gerald's step as he walked on towards the station, tingling with anticipation, living on the edge.

The robbery would be discovered, and sooner or later so would Sheldon's body. The key would be traced, and the loot would be found. The fingerprints on his car would lead them to Vinny and his cronies, and their ridiculous protestations that Sheldon was *not* the man who had run off with their loot would be treated with derision. The perfect murder. And that thought gave Gerald intense pleasure.

As he entered the station, Gerald felt the charge go through his body without 2000 c.c. of engine providing it. *He* was providing it. And he'd show Paula what he could do when he wasn't hung-over and exhausted.

"Security check," said the policewoman. "Could you open your briefcase, please?"

But Gerald couldn't even move.

"If once a man indulges himself in murder, very soon he comes to think little of robbing; and from robbing he comes next to drinking and sabbath-breaking, and from that to incivility and procrastination."

Thomas De Quincey
Murder Considered as One of the Fine Arts

The Changeling

D. W. Smith

It began as a classic story. The paper which started it used the
first issue after Christmas to prod its readers' consciences. The
headline of a double-page spread told them to SPARE A
THOUGHT for people who couldn't enjoy the festivities. A hundred words each on famine, political prisoners, and a victim of
drunk driving surrounded the main item, on a family whose five-
year-old daughter disappeared two days before Christmas. The
paper asked its bloated, gift-laden readers to consider what sort
of day that family had in the house Santa didn't visit.

The TV news took it up. The girl, whose picture was printed,
was reportedly seen that day in a dozen different towns. The
police were filmed conducting house-to-house enquiries. The editor was pleased. It was less gratifying that the following day's
flood of sympathetic letters was accompanied by several ransom
demands. More arrived at the girl's home—some by letter, others by phone. Since the paper had printed the family's name and
home town, it wasn't hard for anybody to get the address and
phone number. Several other families with the same name received similar demands.

The heartlessness of some people, compared to the generosity
of others, became part of the story as it developed. The police
wanted and got volunteers to help search the local countryside.
There were more details about the family. Mona Harris was an
only child. Her father, Bill, forty-four, a senior executive in a
large electronics combine, had a brilliant record in earning ex-

port orders and a reputation for hard work. He'd been married to Brenda, thirty-one, for eight years. They'd lived in their current home for two years, moving there when Bill had joined his present company from a smaller one in the same field. More ransom notes arrived. One included some hair and a piece of her dress. It demanded fifteen thousand pounds, gave the Harrises one day to get the money, and told them to wait by the telephone.

The local CID had already brought in the Regional Crime Squad. The upper echelons conducted a review. They cancelled the search of the countryside and the house-to-house and thought hard about the case's high profile—one national paper campaigning on the story, all the others as well as television and radio reporting it, the family's house besieged by journalists, some of them beginning to flourish their cheque-books. It didn't take long to decide to request help from Scotland Yard.

The file arrived at the desk of Detective Chief Inspector Harry Fathers, who contemplated sending it back. It was obviously going to be one of those cases. True, his section of the Organised Crime Squad had spent most of the year failing to catch a group which ran abduction as a production-line industry. True, too, the snatch had some familiar characteristics. But it didn't have all the hallmarks. And it wasn't the job of the OCS to handle every kidnapping that happened in the realm. But in the end he ignored his instincts and took it on. When asked the obvious question—"Why us?"—he referred to the sensitivity of the case. He omitted to say that he didn't believe that rationalisation himself and that the real reason for accepting the assignment was because he'd just had a major row with his new boss and didn't think he could swing a refusal past him.

"You're not paid to like it or not," he told his DI unsympathetically.

David Pardoner waved a dismissive hand at the file. "They're not my lot," he said. "What this has in common is the target—well off but not fabulously rich—and the size of the ransom—big but not impossible. But my lot don't wait several days before they send the demand in, they don't use the post, and they don't make lurid threats."

"You sound proud of them," said Fathers.

Pardoner shrugged. "You can't deny they're professional," he said. "Got it down to a fine art. This is botched. All the press interest makes it harder for them as well as the target. That delay—not in keeping."

"Well, make what you can of it. I'll get the Press Room to call round the editors and see if they'll call their hounds off. Get down there in strength for the hand-over tomorrow. If you're right it's not down to your lot, maybe we can pick this shower up the easy way."

Pardoner left, still muttering he didn't like it. But it turned out Fathers was right. The kidnappers were caught so easily that the RCS regretted they'd handed the case over. When the back-wash came, though, they decided they'd shown admirable foresight.

The kidnappers' behaviour perfectly bore out Pardoner's derisive view of their incompetence. A voice on the phone told Bill Harris to put the money in a bag, drive to a local park, leave the bag on the bench opposite the big weeping willow, and wait in his car at the nearest exit. The instructions were accompanied by threats of the consequences if he were not alone. He set off and did as he was told. The watching police's telephoto lenses took nice clear pictures of the man who collected the bag and tore off on a spectacularly loud and ill-tuned motorbike. Each of the park's seven exits was covered by a detective in an unmarked car. The motorcyclist's manoeuvrability and acceleration would have made it impossible for one car to follow him, but co-ordinated by Pardoner from the situation room he'd set up in the local police station, the seven took turns and managed it effectively and discreetly. The police helicoptor, booked and ready, wasn't needed. Eventually the motorcyclist stopped at a motorway café and made a phone call.

Harris waited in his car, numb with fear. A man passed, rapped on the window, and handed him a note. More excellent shots were taken of this messenger and the car he went to. There were a couple of unmarked police cars left over, and they managed to pick him and tail him without difficulty. While Harris met more police and drove to the abandoned industrial warehouse where the note said he'd find his daughter, the motorcyclist was being tracked on his way from the café.

Pardoner was ready for as many days of this as it took until the man met other members of the gang or hid the money. But fifteen minutes later he was told the target had arrived at a not very secluded cottage. He ordered all seven cars to converge there, decided to join them, ordered some uniformed assistance and a van to bring the kidnappers back in, and instructed that any visitors could go in but nobody could come out. On his way he was told the messenger had arrived and, a few minutes later, that the girl had been found in the warehouse. She was cold, frightened, shocked, and silent, but otherwise all right, except that her hair had been shaved to the skull. He ordered her to be taken straight home. A medical examination would follow after the family had been reunited.

At the cottage he found some excitement—two men had packed bags in a car. By cutting into the telephone line, he was able to call the occupants of the cottage and announce they were surrounded and should come out quietly. They did so. He was relieved. Even without a hostage, he didn't fancy a siege developing. The other detectives looked sour. They had hoped the kidnappers—there turned out to be three of them—would resist arrest. Nonetheless, the ride back to the police station must have been bumpy because all three arrived with considerable bruises.

The cottage was sealed off and the local scene-of-crime officers summoned to make their minute examination. Nobody could see a real need for it, but Pardoner was a careful investigating officer with a demanding boss. He returned to the police station, thanked the local force for all its assistance, called Fathers to announce a successful conclusion to the case, and prepared to interrogate the arrested men.

And then the backwash hit.

"What do you mean, it's not their daughter?"

Pardoner winced as Fathers' incredulity rasped through the telephone. "Just what I said when Cathy told me."

"What?"

"What you said. She told me it's not their daughter, and I said, what do you mean, it's not their daughter? Just like you. Great minds." Pardoner was trying hard to keep his grip. Flippant irrelevance helped. "The woman took one look at her and screamed," he explained. "Then she said it's not her daughter."

In fact, he was understating to the point of misreporting. Afterwards, Detective Sergeant Cathy Gordon, also trying to keep her grip, adopted hardened cynicism. "Reminded me of that little girl in the William stories," was the way she put it, "who said she'd 'thcweam and thcweam till she wath thick.' Only she didn't threaten, she just did it. Meanwhile, the girl's standing there shaking, the father's standing there shaking, I'm standing there shaking. Finally Mum throws up and after a bit tells the doctor that's not Mona."

"So who is she and where's Mona?" snapped Fathers on the phone.

"You're not the only one who's wondering," Pardoner responded.

"And what does she say? The girl."

"Nowt."

"Shock?"

"Yup—badly. She shivers and shakes and sobs, but nobody's got a word from her yet."

"Not even when you picked her up?"

"Cathy says not. She was there, at the warehouse."

"And the father—what's he say?"

"Likewise nowt."

"Literally?"

"Literally."

"Not even to the little girl, when he saw her?"

"Well, according to Cathy, he said the usual stuff to her at the warehouse, had her on his lap coming back. But since his wife broke the news, silence. He's hitting the bottle. It's puzzling, eh?"

"And maybe not the least puzzling part of it. Hum . . . so where's the girl now?"

"Well, we couldn't really leave her there."

"No."

"So she's on her way to the hospital. They'll put her in the Obbo Ward."

There was a long pause before Fathers' next question: "Do you want me to come down?"

"I wish you would."

"OK. Hold fire on the suspects. Who've you still got there?"

"Nobody's left yet."

"Good. Have 'em hang around. We may need them for the interros if nothing else. Have you got some local plods handy?"

"Droves of them."

"Fine. Look, fax us through a photo of the new girl and physical details. I'll have it put out and about till we pin down where she came from. Had you told the press about your great success?"

"No, thank Christ."

"For one thing at least. OK, I'll be there round six."

When Fathers arrived, the only people in a fit state to be questioned were the kidnappers. Brenda Harris had been given a sedative and was unconscious. So, too, was the little girl she said was not her daughter, in the hospital Observation Ward. Bill Harris was conscious, but drunk. Cathy Gordon had managed to get a family friend to stay with him and returned to the police station leaving two local detective constables in a car outside the house. Fathers got from her a detailed account of everything from the moment the girl had been found, then let every other question hang and started in on the three arrested men.

He took them separately, opening relatively gently each time before belligerently demanding where Mona Harris was and who they'd substituted for her. Uniformly they claimed ignorance of what he meant and denied they'd returned anybody but her. His hectoring scepticism and warnings about the consequences if they persisted in lying had no effect.

With the first round so unproductive, Fathers followed normal procedure and upped the ante. He called in the detectives who were there from his section and more from the local CID and RCS. They were each given a copy of a hastily dictated and typed report.

"That summarises their story so far," he said. "Takes us from the twenty-third, when they snatched Mona, to today when they returned somebody else. What's missing is the when, why, and who of the substitution. They all say it's Mona they handed back. Go through it, hour by hour. When you find something, anything which doesn't gel, step on them. Short of hitting them, anything goes. We badly need one of them to cough."

Now each suspect was under constant interrogation by three detectives who, as they tired, were replaced by another trio. They alternated hard and soft tactics, offered tea, refused it, provided cigarettes and sandwiches which they then threw on the floor, threatened everything from a roughing up to life imprisonment, offered anything from a friendly word in the judge's ear to immediate release on a low bail, appealed to their consciences about the real Mona, went patiently through the details of eight days, jumped forwards and backwards through the accounts, invented things they claimed one of the other suspects had said, contradicted, cajoled, shouted, whispered, pleaded, abused. Fathers circulated from one interview room to another to lend added pressure.

"Can't we just hit him a little bit?" a local detective sergeant, emboldened by weariness, asked in the canteen.

"Happy New Year," Fathers replied and used his cigar to burst a balloon, part of the season's wilting decorations. It was just after midnight.

At four-thirty, one suspect folded gracefully and unconsciously on the floor from utter fatigue. By six, the other two were also asleep in their cells. Eighteen red-eyed detectives joined Fathers to review the case. It didn't take long. There were several discrepancies between the details of the three men's ac-

counts, but on the question of who they had left in the warehouse, they were consistent. It was Mona. Fathers reported the
news—or lack of it—from the Yard. No little girls had been
kidnapped within a hundred and fifty miles and none who
matched the description was missing.

"Right," he said over the moans and grumbles, "shower,
shave, what-have-you, change of clothes, catnap if you must,
then back to it. But this time, go into the background. They've
got no form, and they've not been previously suspected. So:
How'd they get together? Whose idea? Why the Harrises? What
do they know about the family? Before you go, anybody got any
ideas?"

There was only one suggestion. Put diffidently, tiredly, and
anonymously: "Maybe it *is* Mona."

Shortly after lunch, more or less because of that remark, an odd
meeting occurred. It was held at the hospital. Attending it were
three Scotland Yard detectives, the Harris family's GP, the Observation Ward sister, the senior hospital social worker, and two
consultant doctors, one a paediatrician and the other a psychiatrist. Fathers allowed their reports and opinions to ventilate
freely.

"Deep shock," said the paediatrician, "following a huge psy-
chological trauma, including a week's lack of ordinary familial
affection and the total disorientation of incarceration, compli-
cated by an element of mild exposure after being tied up in the
warehouse at subzero temperatures for a couple of hours."

"She doesn't answer when I call her Mona," said the Sister,
"but she won't tell me what her name is either."

"I'm not able," said the psychiatrist, "to comment on either
the girl or the mother. One *possibility*—and I won't go further
than that, it's mere speculation—is that, while the girl's trau-
matised out of normal reactions to family members, the mother
genuinely didn't recognise her because of the shaven head. Under the pressures of the whole affair, which are likely to include
profound guilt—effectively blaming herself for losing the child—

the lack of instant recognition might perhaps harden into rejection. Temporarily at least."

"The only comparable experience I have is reuniting families after a runaway," said the social worker. "It's always difficult and extremely intense. Superexpectation is often followed by disappointment, and then sometimes rejection, before it all settles down. If it does."

"I must say that I can't claim to know her that well," said the GP, "but I did think it was Mona."

"So did the father," said Cathy Gordon. "Otherwise, he'd've said something at the warehouse."

"So why has he changed his mind?" asked Pardoner.

"Indeed, *has* he changed his mind?" asked the psychiatrist.

"Mightn't the answer to either question," the social worker suggested, "depend a lot on what sort of nurturing role he's played in her upbringing?"

"If any," the sister commented acidly.

Cathy Gordon and Fathers exchanged a look. They had interviewed Bill Harris that morning. It had been uncomfortable and difficult. The detectives were tired, impatient, and mentally geared to the hard-driving aggression of the interrogations; it was hard to change pace. Harris was upset, exhausted, and hung-over, barely able to put enough words together to ask them into the sitting room. His wife was upstairs in bed, and he punctuated every hesitant sentence with a glance at the ceiling. The wife of the friend Cathy Gordon had summoned the previous evening was bustling in the kitchen. Finally Fathers asked Harris if he'd prefer it if they went somewhere else to talk.

"To the police station?" Bill Harris asked anxiously.

"I don't see why," said Fathers. "I saw what looked like a nice little café on our way here. Seemed to be open. Might have some decent coffee and cakes or something. I could do with that. Don't know about you."

"Well . . ."

"I'll just go and tell Mrs. Bloomsbury, then," Cathy Gordon said brightly.

In the café, Fathers manoeuvred the interview over the rou-

tine ground of Harris's factual account of the kidnapping and
ransom demand towards the delicate point of when he entered
the warehouse.

"You thought it was Mona then," said Fathers.

It was a full five minutes before Harris replied. "I suppose I
did," he said.

"And up until the point when you got her home."

"I suppose so."

"You had her on your lap, wrapped up in a blanket?"

"Yes."

"So as far as you were concerned, it was Mona."

Harris nodded.

"And now?" asked Fathers.

This time there was a silence of nearly ten minutes. It cost
Fathers a major effort to wait that long. He concentrated on
stopping his right foot from twitching and giving away all the
combined frustration, irritation, sympathy, and impatience he
felt. Finally he couldn't bear it any more. "Well, Mr. Harris," he
said as gently as he could. "What do you think now? Is the girl
you found yesterday in the warehouse Mona or not?"

Harris turned a bleak, despairing gaze on him. But he decided
to speak and, in a fashion, answered.

"It's just so hard, you see," he said. "Brenda seems sure. Sure
she's not. I don't know. You see, I'd actually been away—
abroad. For two months. I only got back late the night before.
On the twenty-second. Business trip. My job takes me away a
lot. And even when I'm here—in the country, I mean. You see,
work's a fair way off. I commute. You know how it is. Leave
early, get back late. There are times when a whole week goes by
without me barely seeing her. Mona. And there can be weekend
things—conferences, extra work, you know. Little children
change so fast. And with her hair all shaved off. Yes. I thought it
was her in the warehouse. But—well, she didn't actually run
into my arms or anything. But, then, I was told to expect she'd
be shocked and so on. Not to expect she'd behave, you know,
normally. And you said she was on my lap on the way back.
That's true, but . . . well, you know, she wasn't really cuddling

into me. But then, I suppose she doesn't really. I mean, you'd probably say we aren't that sort of, well . . . demonstrative. You know. As a family. I mean, it's all all right, we're very loving. But we don't show it very much. Very English, I suppose. And then again, she was cold and probably hadn't been fed very well. I mean, that affected how she looked. She was a bit thinner I suppose. I thought it was her. But Brenda—I have to say it— she knows her better than I do. I mean, naturally. And in the warehouse, you know, nobody said, 'Now is that your daughter, Mr. Harris?' It didn't occur to me. It did to Brenda. I feel awful it didn't. Occur to me. That I don't know her well enough. Well enough to know it wasn't her."

Fathers put a hand on Bill Harris's shoulder. He couldn't think what to say. Cathy Gordon too remained silent.

"What is it to be a good father?" Harris asked suddenly. "How d'you do it?"

"God knows."

"These days, when things are so precarious. You have to give everything you've got to your work. I'm a salesman, you know. Electronics. Pretty high-powered. Hush-hush sort of stuff, selling abroad. I don't work on commission, of course, but it's terribly competitive. Got to keep at it. Ease up and there goes an order. Let things drift and your job's on the line. Income, lifestyle, the lot. I've seen it and I'm not going to let it happen to me. To us. I mean, to be fair, there's a lot I enjoy about it. But it costs, doesn't it? I'd love to be closer to Mona. Really. I was the one who wanted a family. Brenda was for waiting a while. But I'm older than her. I wanted to be young enough to romp around and teach them tennis and things. Brenda was happy enough. I mean, when it happened, she was. She didn't just *go along* with it. But she'd've been happy to wait. I was the one who was keen. But it doesn't work out the way you want or think. Not if you're selling electronics, anyway."

Harris stopped suddenly, as if tripped up by his bathos. He sipped some cold coffee and then continued in a matter-of-fact tone: "Actually I was on a trip in September too. So since we came back from holiday near the end of August, I should think

I've seen her properly for about a week. One week in four
months. Not much in the span of a child that age, is it? You
know that feeling when you can't remember somebody's face
though you've only just seen them? Well then. It was very easy
for me not to realise it wasn't Mona. I have to take Brenda's
word for it."

He paused a long time.

"Don't I?" he added.

At the hospital meeting, Cathy Gordon and Fathers did not
report the interview. But they went over it for Pardoner back in
the same café.

"Works both ways, of course," Pardoner said. "Whether she's
right or wrong, he'll accept her word for it."

"So as far as reliable corroboration goes," said Cathy Gordon,
"forget it!"

"Which means it's down to her mental state," Pardoner continued. "And what we've learned today, among other things, is
that she could be hysterical and simply rejecting her kid, about
whose disappearance she's feeling guilty as hell."

"And whom she wasn't all that sure she wanted to have in the
first place," Cathy Gordon added, "reading between the lines of
what *he* said. And who's been entirely her responsibility while he
cruises off selling electronics here, there, and yonder. Probably
having God knows what fun as he does so. Or at least, leaving
her to wonder where he's dip-sticking. Which, what with AIDS,
is an even less funny thought than it used to be."

"Yes," said Fathers. "Rich brew, isn't it? OK. Cath—to the
Harris's house. Wait there till she's in a state to talk. Just ask
why she knew it wasn't her kid. Don't push her too far. Don't
push her at all, in fact. But it's time to see what she's got to offer.
You, my gentle Pardoner, do what you can to pin this down for
certain—shoe sizes, hair samples, medical records, blood type,
whatever."

"New Year's Day," Pardoner objected. "Bank holiday."

"Stuff that. This is front-page sob story. You saw what it was like at the hospital. They're all prepared to come out for this one. Dig around."

"Confidentially," Pardoner added.

Fathers gave him a look, then caught a frown on Cathy Gordon's face. "What's your problem?" he asked her.

"Just thinking about the shaven-head business. Wondering why they did it. They didn't send all the hair to the family after all."

"What'd the shrink say?" mused Fathers. "Transferred self-mutilation? I liked that."

"I thought it might be more like the B and E merchants who crap on the best rug before they go," commented Pardoner.

Cathy Gordon shrugged. "Maybe," she said, "but motives aren't always irrational."

The sedative had worn off. Brenda Harris had refused another, pacifying the doctor with a promise to accept one that night. Her sad features sparked with quickly snuffed hope when Cathy Gordon arrived. She was prepared to answer questions, but there was really just one question—"Are you still sure that's not Mona?"—and it only needed to be repeated once for her to see what the detective was driving at.

"You think I'm hysterical," she said flatly. "Well, why not? You saw me being hysterical. Even so. Isn't it all so typical? The police are baffled, as they say, so blame it on the bloody woman, who's probably barmy and doesn't know her own mind what with all the pressure."

Cathy Gordon shook her head. "You don't sound barmy to me, Mrs. Harris. Angry, but not crazy."

"Huh! I can see it in your eyes. You're thinking about all the pressure. First Mona disappears, then all the publicity, the police, then the ransom note. You're probably even quite sympathetic about it, so understanding!"

Cathy Gordon was silent. The bitterness was uncomfortably accurate.

"But it still comes down to the same thing, doesn't it? That the poor woman's off her rocker."

"No, look, please listen."

"Why should I? When you've come here to persuade me I'm off my head, when you should be out finding Mona."

"That's not at all why I'm here. If you just think back to yesterday afternoon, and remember you only saw her for a second and consider—"

"One thing, since he won't talk to me, what's Bill say?"

"—that she'd be bound to look very different—"

"Not that it matters what he says."

"—not least because of her hair being shaven off—"

"He can tell a thirty-two-bit chip from a sixteen-bit by smell alone—"

"—and with the shock and cold, and probably not having eaten much—"

"—but not his own daughter from a total stranger."

"—then it would be hardly surprising if you didn't—"

"Mr. Got-to-get-ahead-at-all-costs Bill Harris."

"Oh the hell with it. Are you going to bloody listen or not?"

"No."

"Why were you so sure it wasn't Mona? You only had a second."

"For Christ's sake," Brenda Harris snapped. "What sort of question is that?"

"Mrs. Harris, please, I'm trying to understand."

"Are you?" said Brenda Harris. "And are you a mother?"

"No."

"Then you can't understand."

"Tell me. Please."

Brenda Harris looked at the detective for a while. Finally she shook her head and said, "I'll try, though I really don't believe you can understand. Look, I *know* her—her eyes, the way she walks and holds herself, her gestures, everything. I don't need her sodding hair to know. I don't need her rosy cheeks and smile. I've nursed her through night fevers. I've seen her happy, sad, and everything in between. I know Mona. And that girl, whoever she is, poor little thing, is not Mona."

Cathy Gordon looked steadily at Brenda Harris and their eyes engaged.

"Do you think I don't wish it was Mona? Do you think I'm not jumping out of my skin wanting it to be her? What do you think? I *expected* it to be Mona. One of your lot phoned up, said, 'We've got Mona, we'll be back in a few minutes.' I was all ready for this whole thing, this . . . this hell . . . ready for it to be over. And then it wasn't. Look, I literally would give absolutely anything for that little girl to be Mona, but it's not."

Cathy Gordon nodded thoughtfully. The other woman paused, then asked, "You don't know who she is, the girl?"

"We're looking. Nobody's come forward yet."

"What does she say?"

"Nothing. She's in deep shock."

"Poor thing. And what about *her* mother?" Brenda Harris shook her head again. "What do you think? Will Mona come back?"

"Yes."

"Huh. You'd have to say that. I wonder what you really reckon the chances are. Less than fifty-fifty and fading?"

"We don't deal in odds. We do what we can."

"Yes," said Brenda Harris with bitter mock brightness. "Best thing. On with the job. Talking of which, what does Bill say, anyway?"

"Says he doesn't see enough of his daughter."

"Too bloody true."

"That he'd like to see more of her."

"Precious little sign he ever gives of it."

"Says he trusts your word."

"Oh. Well, I suppose—if he can't trust his own. But you can't find Mona. And what do they say? Whoever took her."

"That she's Mona."

Brenda Harris looked away. "Well, that was a straight answer. I can see how it goes. You've given them a rough time. Asked them everything you can think of. Probably kicked them a few times, though we know that doesn't go on, don't we? But they still tell the same story, so you've begun to believe it. Meanwhile, the little girl's a mystery. So the next thing is, check the woman out and see whether she's dropped any marbles. Looked at from your point of view, it's reasonable enough."

Cathy Gordon shook her head. "It's not like that," she said. It was only half a lie. It was why she was there. But it was not what she thought now. She took a deep breath and decided to try again. "You're not barmy, Mrs. Harris. But will you come to the hospital . . . ?"

"What're you going to do? Show me ink blots?"

"Show you the little girl. Ask you to tell me again that you're sure."

"You say I'm not barmy but you don't—"

"Look, don't start up again, just don't. What've you got to lose?"

Brenda Harris looked out of the window. "Nothing," she said finally.

At the hospital, she stood in silent tears gazing at the little girl tucked up asleep on the other side of the observation window. At length she turned to the woman detective and shook her head. "No," she said.

Fathers grimaced at the folders on his desk in the situation room —reports on the interrogations. But two hours spent reading them produced a sort of illumination. One of the discrepancies between the kidnappers' stories concerned who had cut the girl's hair off and when. At first, his mind focused on where Mona was, why she'd been substituted, and by whom. It had seemed a minor detail which could be sorted out later, but the brief exchange about it in the café had stirred a thought or two. He ploughed through the scene-of-crime report and made brief notes on two things. One was a footprint outside, too large to be made by any of the three who'd been arrested. The other was something it didn't mention—hair clippings on the floor, on chairs, in the rubbish, anywhere—though it did report a bagful of tresses. The man who'd written the report was the region's senior scene-of-crime officer. Fathers phoned him and, as tactfully as he could, checked that he had in fact looked for stray hair clippings. It wasn't tactful enough. "Course I bloody did, what d'you think?" was the reply. Being a DCI, he had the freedom to address the Scotland Yard man like that.

Fathers shrugged and got an unoccupied constable to check the weather reports of the past week. He phoned the Yard and learned that nowhere within three hundred miles had there been a likely-looking kidnap or runaway. "Keep going," he said. "When you've covered the country, try Interpol." Then Cathy Gordon called from the hospital to say the mother still claimed —and convincingly—that the little girl wasn't Mona.

He went to the canteen for some coffee and a smoke. He had a muddy case, no time, and a sort of opening. It seemed best to chance his arm. He thought about the kidnappers and how they had responded to the interrogations. One of them had acted particularly tough and had been broken especially well by Pardoner. He'd spent most of the time sobbing. Realisation of what he had got into—of the risks—had hit him hard, but too late. He was the best bet. Fathers had him brought to an interview room and gave him a cup of tea and a pack of cigarettes.

"Andrew Brice," he said quietly, "age thirty-nine, resident of Southampton, unemployed, previously a garage hand, made redundant, no previous arrests or convictions. And in over your head."

Brice was stubbornly silent.

"It's more serious than you know," Fathers added. "To me, this looks like more than kidnapping, though that's serious enough. I'm talking murder."

"Rubbish," sneered Brice. "You're trying it on." He sounded confident, recovering the hard poise with which he'd started the previous night, but the tea which spilled into his saucer told a different story.

"No, it's no try on. The girl you handed back isn't Mona. We don't know who she is, but we'll find out. Meanwhile, the question is, where's Mona?"

"You keep going on about it, you lot, but I've told you a thousand times, she's Mona Harris all right, she bloody is."

Brice's voice rose sharply at the end of the sentence. "Why'd she be anybody else?"

"We haven't found the body," Fathers continued smoothly, "and maybe we won't. But it's not necessary, you know. There's precedent for murder convictions without a body being discovered."

Brice lit a cigarette. Fathers hid his pleasure at the shaking hand which held the match. "Murder means life," he said quietly, "and more and more judges are saying that when they sentence someone to life, they mean it. Kidnap brings down a pretty long stretch, of course, but not a real life term, not usually. And child-killers don't get an easy time inside."

"What you're saying, it's just talking nonsense."

"Oh, you'd better believe me, I wouldn't do that. I might fit you up a bit, but I wouldn't talk nonsense."

"I'll tell 'em you said that."

"Tell the world. The tape's not running."

"You can't do it."

"Your trouble is, you don't take me seriously. I could send you down for whatever I put my mind to. You probably haven't had enough experience to know that. But you can believe it if I tell you. Can't you?"

Brice looked into the policeman's eyes for a second. The quiet, unemphatic threats were cutting through his confidence even more sharply than all the bullying.

"But you do have a way out. If you give us a little help. I've got three questions. I want honest answers. I want them now. No second chance. I'm asking you because I think you may be just smart enough to see you've no choice but to answer them. Number one, why'd you shave her head?"

"What do you think? So her family'd know we meant business."

"Number two, when did you do it?"

"At the cottage, soon after we got her there."

"That's a lie. You're not taking me seriously still. And number three, there was somebody else at the cottage, a fourth man. Who?"

"Nobody."

"You're lying again. He left a footprint. In the mud when we had that rain, preserved by the frost. Who?"

"Nobody."

"Who the fuck do you think we are?" Fathers shouted. "Who was it?!"

"No, he never came there!" Brice shouted back.

Fathers smiled benignly and allowed Brice to realise what he'd said. "Shall we begin from the beginning?"

Brice took his time. Fathers allowed him to. The story came out eventually.

"He said there was some bastard done him down. Wanted to get back at him. Told us what to do. We were to get all the money, he wasn't interested in it. He picked the girl up, told us her name, address, and phone. He delivered her to us. On the road from the motorway to the cottage. Then we had to wait a few days to let him get clear before we sent the ransom demand. He'd already shaved her hair off. It was in a bag. Said to send some of it so they knew we were serious."

"He put you all up to it, did he?"

"Yeah, it was his idea. He said if anything went wrong, to leave him out of it. He had a way. You knew he'd get you if you dumped him in it."

Fathers nodded. The threat must have been very powerful for its effect to survive everything but his own threat of a rigged murder charge—and even then Brice had not wanted to give him away.

There were no celebrations afterwards. When Fathers got home late the next day, he took his sleeping children in his arms and hugged them for a long time. They woke up and looked at him wonderingly. He said nothing, kissed them back to sleep, and after a bit tucked them up again. He gave Sarah a brief outline of the case as he opened the whisky. She shook her head sadly, accepted a drink, stayed with him for the second one, and then went to bed while he sat alone and got bitterly drunk.

Brice hadn't known the man's name, but one of the others did.

They had worked for a time in the same company until it went out of business. He'd been the point of contact. The name led to an address in Southampton and a visit from the local police. They found a large house, untidy and uncared for inside, and a corpse. Beside it they found a typewritten page. It answered all the questions of who, why, and where. It explained who the little girl in the Observation Ward was and, though not explicitly, the depths of her shock. It described everything it was relevant to know so the file could be closed, including what had happened to Mona. It was why success gave Fathers nothing to be happy about.

Did you think you would get away with it? I've always known how you bought your way into that nice big safe company when you left us. You're good enough at selling, but what interest would they have in you except for that? Saved them millions in development money and gave them a market lead.

I don't just resent that you stole it, but you stole it from *me*. My work, my idea, my sweat. And it's not even just that. It shouldn't be used that way. Fuck you Harris with all your cleverness and industry—I made a home security aid for the newly blind and you twisted it into cut-price IFF for all-weather combat aircraft.

But there's more: when your company put its social hat on and went out to sell it as a blind aid too, its price was naturally better than ours—economy of scale and no development money to recover—so we went bust.

BUST. I don't think you'll ever know what that means. You're one of those slimes who'll always be successful because you'll do anything and pay any price.

Any price? Well, we can see about that.

My life of course—and not just mine—went down the drain. So that's where you go.

Out of pride more than anything. I'd fake an accident if I had any life insurance left, and leave the kid something. But I cashed it all in trying to keep life going as normal. When it ran out and life got to be subnormal, Sylvia left. You remember her—my wife, the one you chatted up that time. She took Alice. I can't blame her, nor regret them going. I didn't much like either one by the end.

You'll say, pull yourself together—or something equally bizarre and stupid. Get another job. Pick yourself up. A cliché for every occasion, that's how I remember you from before you learnt how to cheat. But why should I pull myself together? To compete in your world? No bloody thanks. I've had enough.

But I don't see either why I should just fade quietly away.

So I've put together a gang of no-hopers and lined them up with a plan. It begins with kidnapping your little girl.

It always struck me how alike yours and mine were.

Alice is with me for Christmas while her mother swans off with a new man to the Canaries. Sylvia's dug her way out. That was predictable, I suppose. She's more your sort than mine in some ways. She's going to get a lesson too.

Just at the moment, I'm enjoying all the press coverage and TV. I hope you're suffering. There's worse to come. I've swapped them. My crew of nobodies don't know that. I've cut their hair off. Some of your girl's will be sent to you. But the daughter you're getting back today isn't yours. She's coming with me when I go. And I reckon that, with her hair cut off, Alice will look enough like Mona to fool you for a while, long enough to make you realise what a shit you are.

You can't cheat your way out of this one. Sort it out for yourself. Learn the price of success. And rot.

Well, that *was* the plan. I went to do it. And I couldn't. Despite her father, what's she got to be blamed for? And I'm afraid she looks too much like Alice. I could go so far— but not the whole way. So I've just locked her away, with some food and warm clothes. Out in the garage.

You'll get her back. Feel how lucky you are. Bastard.

Stone Mother

Jean Stubbs

I am walking into this village very early on a summer morning, and as I pass by the church, the trees overhang the wall and scatter sunlight on me like a blessing. I could do with blessing, and that's for sure, but we must deal with life as best we can, and if my way of dealing broke a few rules then this is the time to turn over a new leaf. The day is not properly awake. The outlines of the cottages on my right are hazy, and the fields about them are pale with mist. This is a tranquil little place, the sort of place for a man to retire to and bury his past.

I reach the end of the street, climb the stile, and jump down on to the other side, to face a vista of open moorland inhabited only by sheep and stones. The mist is thick about my feet, and as I walk along the grassy track, I find the remnants of a pattern in the stones. Most of them are mere stumps; some lean at an angle; the missing ones leave obvious gaps, like teeth in an old mouth. I consult the map on the back of the property details which the estate agent gave me yesterday, turn away from the path, and follow another grass track into a grove of trees on my left. For an instant my heart leaps into my throat. Then I laugh at myself because it is only another stone, which the mist has obscured so that its worn surface is no longer visible, and its shape resembles a hooded woman holding a child.

Here the grove ends but the track continues, trailing down into a hollow, and on the hillside opposite is the place I have come to view. I pause at the garden gate before I lift the latch.

I should find Stonehouse well built, the estate agent said. A handsome property in eighteenth-century style and proportions, but somewhat neglected. Though the price is reasonable and the property has great potential, it has been empty for quite a while. Why? I asked. He said he thought the situation was too lonely for most people. It was impossible to reach by car, which ruled out elderly folk and young families. On the other hand, it was a large house, which tended to put off single buyers. The last tenants had been a middle-aged married couple, but the wife died and the husband was unhappy by himself. Still, if you are looking for a secluded property, the agent said, this is ideal. Oh, and the garden is large but somewhat overgrown, he added as an afterthought.

The mist is beginning to clear, and I see that the garden is a wilderness. Now the sun comes out, and at the end of a tangle of brambles that used to be a path, the windows of the house stare out at me with blind bright eyes and I recognise it as my own. It is a house that holds secrets and keeps its own counsel. A house that will close and bar its doors against those it does not want. A house without near neighbours, fit for a solitary man.

I take out the key which the agent has given me, and turn it in the lock of a dark stout door. I open the door and go in. No one has been here for a very long time. There is a smell of damp, a lifting of dust, echoes, and emptiness. But as I look round I see it as it will be in a year's time, rich in my possessions. So far I have lived comfortably but modestly, for if a man rides in a gold carriage, he must expect to be robbed. But now I can bring out the treasures I have accumulated and stored over the years.

Upstairs and down I walk, slow and sure, running my penknife into suspect wood, peering into all the places the agent would not like me to see, missing nothing in the long list of neglect. I shall spend the morning here, acting as my own surveyor. For I started life as the son of a bricklayer, who tried to make a bricklayer out of me. But I found that I was quicker, cleverer, and more ambitious than my father's son should have been. He was a good man who worked hard all his life and died poor. So I looked about me and took every opportunity offered, and made a few for myself, until I had a thriving little building business, which became a bigger business. Then I found easier work with richer pickings. No questions asked and none answered. I learned about corrupt town councils and contracts and a few other things, but I always made sure my tracks were covered, and I earned a reputation for high-quality workmanship and reliability.

I helped my parents as much as my father would let me, but when he died, I looked after the old lady for ten years in the way I wanted to, and she had the best time of her life. She was the only woman I ever trusted.

I learned in my kind of life that it was best to travel alone, so I never married. I liked women, make no mistake about it, but I kept them in a compartment labelled PLEASURE. I could always get a woman when I wanted one, and we followed the same routine every time. I told her nothing, treated her well, gave her a generous present when I was tired of her, and made sure she understood that the affair was over for good. I never had any trouble with any of them.

And now this is my time, the time I have worked and planned for, and I am going to enjoy it. No pressures from other people. No looking over my shoulder. A quiet life with a few acquaintances to liven it here and there, and the chance to do things I have never done before. Because there's another side to me, apart from the rough-and-tough bit, and I'm going to give it a chance.

I scribble a few calculations on the back of the agent's brochure and make a few more in my head. I have no intention of paying the price that is being asked, though this is exactly what I want. Exactly. I take one final look round before I go. The house is like me—a rough diamond. Well, I shall make us both shine.

We have been most interested in our new neighbour and his acquisition of Stonehouse, which has been understandably vacant these last few years. I wonder whether he knows the history of the house? Probably not. The estate agents were only too pleased to get it off their hands, even at the price I hear he paid them. Anyway, he is living rough there for the moment and doing much of the restoration work himself, with the help of our local odd-job man, Don Fowler. According to Don, our friend is generous with money but not an easy man to work for, being fiendishly exact about every detail.

This morning I called on him in my capacity of parish priest, though I must admit that curiosity drew me quite as much as good fellowship, and I found him brewing tea in the chaos of his future kitchen.

He looked up in a genial manner, waved a hand at a packing case, dropped another tea-bag in the pot, and said, "Sit down, Reverend. Milk? Sugar?"

And as soon as we had a mug in our hands, he sat down opposite me and gave me his full attention. I must say that I found him immensely likeable on first acquaintance and a fascinating character.

He introduced himself as Harry Bean. I guessed him to be in his early fifties. He must have been a handsome fellow in his youth and was still a good-looking man with a head of iron grey curly hair, well above average height, and built like a boxer. His face was high-coloured and clean-shaven, his sharp brown eyes looked directly into mine, and he chatted away as easily as if we had known each other for years. I heard all about his humble parentage, his former business upcountry, his present plans and future hopes, and his desire to "better" the house and himself. All this was recounted with the utmost good humour and accompanied by a rumbling laugh. He was no hypocrite either, no beater about the bush. He said outright that he respected my cloth and my beliefs but did not share them, being by experience and conviction an agnostic. I was not surprised by this. More and more do I believe that the church is in decline. We fight a rearguard action against present-day materialism and immorality. And here, in this remote village, I have more ancient problems to contend with. So he and I spoke of general things, finding a common interest in good claret, cricket, chess, ancient myths and history, and the fact that we were both bachelors by choice.

"I have always found the church demanding enough, without the distraction of a family," I said. "And though the lack of a wife has been something of a drawback—women are so good at managing the social side of church work!—still I have an excellent and devoted housekeeper. And the ladies of the parish are only too anxious to help me out—though that too can be a drawback at times!"

"I'm a loner myself," he said. "So that makes two of us. Well, Reverend, as soon as this place is shipshape you must come over one evening and share a bottle of claret and a game of chess."

I was interested. I was flattered. Invitations usually fell into two categories: either people asked me as a matter of duty, or they wanted something of me and sweetened their request with hospitality. This man simply desired my company.

I said, half joking, "Are you not afraid that I shall try to convert you, Mr. Bean?"

He laughed and replied, "Don't try unless you relish a good argument with no holds barred. I do nothing without reason, and though you probably went to public school and university, and I'm only self-educated, I've read a lot and I'm prepared to argue the hind leg off Balaam's ass!"

I thought that rather a neat remark and laughed myself. As a student, I used to be a keen debater, but that was a side of me which has had to remain neglected. My somewhat solitary nature has brought me to solitary places which are devoid of intellectual argument. In desperate straits I have been known to put a knotty point or two to the Lord—may He forgive me—but He is another non-debater.

"That will be a change," I said and found myself rubbing my hands. "I shall accept that invitation, Mr. Bean!"

As I stood up to leave, I looked up through his kitchen window and saw the stone image watching over his house. It was not a prospect I should have relished myself, but he seemed unperturbed and asked me if I did not think it was intended to be a woman and child.

"It may have been carved that way, or it may be a trick of

weathering," I replied, "but the resemblance is certainly there. She is known hereabouts as Stone Mother."

He stroked his chin thoughtfully, as if he had once worn a beard. "It could be the Virgin and Child, but I suppose it's too old to be Christian."

"Too old by a couple of thousand years, I should say. It was once part of a huge circle, which has been practically destroyed. There has been a history of witchcraft and paganism in this part of the world, and most of the stones were dug up in the name of Christianity, split apart, and used for mending walls and farms in the eighteenth century. Stone Mother, regarded as a fertility symbol, was apparently buried by her devotees and resurrected in kindlier times. Nowadays all the stones are under the protection of the Department of the Environment. As a national monument, the circle is too damaged to arouse a great deal of interest, and I am glad that this is so. I should be sorry if our village attracted the attentions of a horde of tourists or a hippie gathering on Midsummer Night's Eve, augmented by policemen . . ."

"Is there a story attached to this Stone Mother?"

"The experts reckon that she must have been a stone of great power for the local people to have saved her. Possibly a heathen goddess. There are many stories about the fate of people who mutilated or destroyed the stones, though I don't know how true they are. But even now, I am sad to say, some of the village brides and infertile women and mothers-to-be, at certain times of the year and at certain hours, will secretly lay offerings at the Stone Mother's feet—wheat ears at harvest time, flowers in spring and summer. There is a strong pagan streak in these people still and something worse than that hereabouts. Black magic, Mr. Bean. The Devil has his devotees. We had one unpleasant incident a few years ago when they held a meeting inside the circle and made a blood sacrifice. Fortunately, only a sheep . . ."

I did not want to be asked questions about his house, so I said, "This has been most pleasant, but I must leave you to your labours and carry on with my own."

But he said, "I know I can have the truth from you, Reverend, because of your calling. And you needn't be afraid of speaking out. I don't scare easily and I'm not superstitious. I haven't been here very long, but I'm an observant sort of bloke. What is there that worries people about this house?"

I hesitated a moment, but felt compelled to tell the truth.

"I believe that some of the stones were used to lay the foundations, and I am bound to confess that the house has had an unfortunate history. Scandals of various kinds. Black magic has been practised here. The last owner was suspected of helping his wife to die, though nothing was proven. In fact, it was empty so long this time that there was talk of pulling it down."

"So I've given it a new lease of life then, Reverend?"

"Oh yes. You could certainly say that."

"Then that's a good thing, isn't it? A charitable thing? To give somebody—or something—a second chance?"

I had to agree, though I had my reservations about his choice of charity. He shook my hand affably and showed me to the door, saying, "Well, Reverend, you won't see me at church, but I wish the church well. If it needs any money for upkeep, you have only to ask me."

I hesitated to impose upon such a brief acquaintance, but we were struggling to raise a fund for the roof before it fell about our ears. I mentioned our efforts.

He grinned outright and asked, "How much have you collected so far?"

"Three hundred and twenty-five pounds and sixty-seven pence."

"And how much do you need?"

"Five thousand for a new roof. Five hundred for immediate repair."

He went over to a tea-caddy on the mantelshelf and took out a roll of notes.

"I can't go the whole hog," he said, "but I can make up the difference."

And he peeled four fifty-pound notes from the roll, which seemed hardly diminished by the gift.

"My goodness me!" I said, quite winded by the gesture and

the amount. "Oh, my goodness me. This is extraordinarily . . . well, I don't know what to say." I felt bound to say something nevertheless. "You will forgive my mentioning the matter, Mr. Bean, but is it entirely wise, even in these remote parts, to keep so much money in the house?"

"This house is the safest place for all my possessions, Reverend," he said, returning the notes to their japanned hiding place. "And I can take care of it and myself." He smiled to soften the statement and added, "Thank you, all the same."

I felt my calling strong upon me in that place, with the Stone Mother looking down upon us. In spite of his agnosticism, I said, "I shall pray for you, Mr. Bean."

But he answered sincerely, with an earnestness which I found amusing.

"I'll be glad of that. Always back a horse both ways, I say. You never know when a prayer might come in handy. And drop in again, Reverend, any time."

I did call again, partly because he had asked me and partly because I wanted to. He was quite the most interesting person for miles around and I have been lonely here, and occasionally fearful, but Harry Bean and I spent many an enjoyable hour as he turned the truth inside and out and I countered him warmly.

One particularly entertaining winter tea the debate lasted so long that it turned to supper, and the clock struck ten before we noticed. It was one of those strange nights when this county enters another world and the moon rides high and everywhere is still and even the stones and trees are listening to something we cannot hear. The cattle are restless, dogs bark, and civilisation is unwelcome. And here, where the house had been built on a foundation of broken images, the pagan force was strongest. I stared up at the Stone Mother and lingered a few reluctant moments on his threshold before pitting my spiritual strength against hers, and he seemed to read my mind.

"Should you like me to walk with you as far as the stile?" he asked, grinning. And on being refused—a little pettishly, I fear —he said humorously, "Then keep to the straight and narrow on the way home, Reverend. There are older gods than yours abroad tonight!"

Over the next twelve months, he transformed a derelict, unloved heap of stones into a comfortable home, and there led the life of a comfortable hermit. A local woman came in one day a week to clean and took his washing home with her, but he kept the house as well and as graciously as any woman could. He was something of a fanatic about physical fitness. He joined a judo class, an art in which he was apparently quite proficient. We saw him running and jogging. And whatever the weather, he would walk briskly to the village every day around lunchtime, haversack on back, to pick up his newspaper and milk and post, and buy a few necessities from the general shop. He rented a garage in the village for his car, because there was no way to reach his place except—as the village folk say—by four legs or two.

His routine became predictable. Once a week he drove out to the nearest market town, spent the day there, and did the bulk of his shopping. On Saturdays he passed an amiable evening at the pub, playing darts, standing drinks, and chatting. Occasionally he invited three or four of the local men over for a game of cards. Sometimes he went fishing with one or two of them. But he didn't fit into any particular group, being too sophisticated for the villagers and too unpolished for the gentry. So he made no friends apart from myself, and he never had any visitors from outside. Still, his life was pleasant enough. He seemed busy and contented. And he was studying for O-levels in his spare time. "Bettering" himself, as he would have said. He was a remarkable man.

The vicarage is a receiving station for local news. What is not confided to me is whispered to my housekeeper, Betty Hocking, and I am still astonished by the amount of knowledge the country grapevine garners and passes on. So my breakfast was enlivened by a story that our local pub, named the Green Man, had had a mysterious visitor the previous evening: a dapper little man who left his Rolls-Royce in the car-park and gave the landlord a five-pound tip to make sure that it was safe. He had bought and drunk a double brandy and asked about the stone circle, saying he was interested in such things. He was very up-country, they said, quite the city gentleman. So they advised him to come back by daylight, when he could see the stones better, and gave him the name of Harry Bean, since he was living nearby. He said that he had a torch and would take a quick look round anyway, because he might not be coming back this way for a while—at which Mrs. Hocking said, "Sooner him than me at that time of night, and with them stones!"—and he thanked them and left. Nobody saw him again, and with his car still being there at closing time, they wondered whether to call the police. But they thought the better of it, and the car had gone by morning, though nobody saw it go.

"My word, Mr. Bean and I will have something to talk about tomorrow night!" I said, for that was our usual evening to enjoy a game of chess.

So I arrived a little early at Stonehouse and entered with my customary lack of ceremony, for we were accounted good friends by this time and he left his door unlocked. Usually he was waiting for me in the sitting room with the chessboard laid ready, but this evening he called to me from the dining room, and I found him finishing his supper in solitary state. As usual, he had changed his jeans and jersey for a well-cut grey suit and a tie and replaced his sneakers with polished black shoes.

The house was looking very grand these days, and although he was alone, he had laid the table with precise attention to detail. Materially speaking, my childhood was more fortunate than my manhood, and the appearance of the room aroused nostalgia. In such a fashion had my parents dined in pre-war years. Only a parlour maid was missing. But his cleaning lady had done her work well, and my attention was caught first by the high polish of the silverware and then by its elegance.

"All Georgian," he said, not boastfully but reverently, and gave me a brief and articulate sermon on each piece.

For a while he was animated, but when the silver had been thoroughly discussed, he apparently lost interest. His usual geniality had vanished. His mood was dark. His composure sat heavily upon him.

In order to break the silence, I said, for I had never seen him at table, "Is today a special occasion? Or do you dine like this every evening?"

He brightened up again momentarily.

"No special occasion, Reverend. When I was a lad I ate from oilcloth, and the only ornament on the table was the tomato sauce bottle. Nowadays I like to live up to what I've got. You must come and join me one evening. Can't think why I didn't ask you before—except that my cooking's nothing out of the ordinary. Still, I'm taking a night class in *haute cuisine* this winter . . ."

He remembered his duties as a host, and rose and took another coffee cup and saucer from the sideboard cupboard.

"Black or white, Reverend?"

"Oh, white please."

"Shall we take it into the sitting room with us, along with the brandy bottle?"

"By all means, my friend."

The fire had been lit long since, providing both warmth and living beauty on a cold November night. We sat down and made ourselves comfortable.

He said at random, "I learned early on not to trust anybody but myself." He was silent, thinking, and then asked, "Sugar, Reverend?"

To my dismay, I recognised the signs of an imminent confession.

"Two, please." I cleared my throat and said cheerfully, "Learning *not* to trust your fellow men seems to be a pretty bleak philosophy, Harry."

"It's a bleak world," he said doggedly. "I deal with it on its own terms." He looked at me directly, saying, "But I can trust you, Reverend, because of your calling. That's right, isn't it?"

I looked longingly at the chessboard, for I was burdened daily with other people's troubles and could seldom unburden my own, but I knew my duty.

"Anything you tell me will be safe with me, if that's what you mean, Harry."

He sat there, a big, handsome, unsmiling man, rich in worldly goods.

"I'll deal straight with you, Reverend. My life hasn't been all it should be, but I hadn't a lot of choice, and as soon as I could make it right, I did. You'll bear me out in that, I hope? I've done no harm here, have I?"

"None that I know of, Harry."

"I've done none, Reverend. My word on that. And you can bear witness that I've tried to better myself in every way."

"I know you have, Harry," I answered, somewhat puzzled. "And if the past is behind you and you've turned over a new leaf, then all is well."

"What would you say if I told you that somebody wanted to turn that new leaf back again? Wanted me to go back to my old ways?"

"I should advise you most strongly to resist the temptation," I said firmly.

"There's no temptation, Reverend. I could go on the way I am until I drop dead. And I'll leave your church a nice fat sum in my will too. Buy a few prayers, just in case." He looked inward on his darkness and said more to himself than to me, "We can all make mistakes. I'd like to think I was covered."

I answered somewhat stiffly, "Prayers cannot be bought and would in any case be freely given."

He said sincerely, "You're a good man, Reverend." But his guard was down, and though he spoke to me, I still felt it was an inner dialogue with himself.

"I can understand goodness in simple people—they've got nothing to think with—but not in clever ones. I've often wondered why someone of your intelligence ended up in a back o'beyond place like this, pottering round the farms and cottages, when he could have been an archbishop."

"An archbishop? Oh, come, come! You rate me too highly, my friend," I said briskly, feeling disquieted.

He was ruminating in deadly earnest.

"Of course, if it had been me in your shoes, I'd have chosen the Church of Rome. They deal with the world as it is, not as it should be. Very well thought out. The confessional. The show-manship. All that gold. And I'd have gone high. Not to the top. I don't say that. I reckon you have to be something extra to be pope. But near. Yes, very near."

His affable manner and open smile had gone. This was a man to be feared. Uneasily, I imagined him in a cardinal's robes, surrounded by a king's ransom of gold images, manipulating, plotting. The thought chilled me.

"For what purpose?" I asked coldly.

"My own. It'd be safer than some of the things I've had to do."

His mood changed. He poured out the brandy and grinned at my uneasiness.

"Life is what you make it, Reverend. I've always chosen to make it work for me." He waved his hand to indicate the rich-ness of his possessions, saying, "How do you think I came by all these. I'll tell you something in confidence, Reverend. Not all of them were bought."

His face relaxed. He had found out how to begin.

"Remember what I said about trusting people? Well—present company and my parents excepted—that was right. Thirty years ago I was a young man with no money, no connections, and plenty of ambition. I knew what I wanted, but I didn't know how to get it. Then somebody—we'll call him Benny, for the sake of a name—took a fancy to me and did me a favour. He bought up a small family building firm which was going broke, and put me in to manage it. We did it in a businesslike way, drew up a proper contract. I aimed to buy the business for myself in time, and I paid him interest on the loan. He was very influential was Benny, and he put one or two contracts my way. I was green in those days, and I swallowed them before I realised they were bait. I built that business up and bought it from him and made it thrive. But what I didn't realise was that he'd got something on me, and I couldn't refuse what he wanted me to do. A builder, you see, gets to know quite a bit about other people and their property, and I could find things out that were useful to him.

"He ran a little empire of his own did Benny, and he wasn't

too particular about what he did. A catholic taste in crime as you might say. And he knew how to make people work for him. He paid his men—and women—well, and if they had to do a stretch, then he looked after their families and found them a job when they came out. No one talked and no one ever said no. It wasn't worth their while.

"He had two faces, one public—you'd be surprised if I gave you his proper name!—and one private. He was a smooth-looking, smooth-talking, little bastard who enjoyed the good life, and he knew a lot of rich and influential people. The police have had an eye on him for years. They never found a way of nailing him.

"So I went along with him because I had to. If he ever liked anybody, it was me. I made him laugh, you see. He used to say I was the brother he never had. And I was smart and I was cunning. I never saw the inside of a clink, and he never had to bail me out. I used my wits and kept my head above water for over thirty years, but I'd no intention of staying under his bloody thumb for life.

"Benny didn't like people leaving him. So I had to think up a good story. I told him I'd been given my cards—a bad heart condition—and would have to retire. I said I was thinking of taking a long holiday abroad. I don't know whether he believed me or not, but it was a face-saver for him. Then I waited for the right moment. It came while he was cruising in some millionaire's yacht round the Mediterranean. I sold my business as soft and quick as a whistle in the dark and went. I left him a friendly letter saying I'd be in touch—a promise that I never meant to keep.

"I always knew how to cover my tracks. For a month or two I moved from place to place, getting deeper into the West Country, looking round for somewhere quiet to settle. And there were plenty of places, but something here, something about this house, drew me as nothing else had done. The house was like me, you see. It had started out wrong, but it needed a second chance. And I've made it shine. You have to admit that, Reverend. I've made it shine. The last fourteen months have been the best in my life.

"By the way, Reverend, my name isn't Harry Bean, but there's no point in telling you the real one. It's as well not to know too much. I say that for your own good. You're an innocent, you see, Reverend, meaning no disrespect."

He offered me another cognac, which I accepted.

"Then Benny found me. It took him over a year, but he found me. He came here last night. I opened the door, thinking it was you, and he walked in as if he owned the place, saying, *Hiding from something, my boy? New name. New face.* I'd shaved off my beard, you see. And then he said, straight from the heart, *Why choose a God-forsaken hole like this? I nearly lost a shoe getting here!*

"If it wasn't so awful it'd be funny. To think of Benny finding his way among those stones in his patent leather shoes, and only a pocket torch between him and the dark! Laugh? You could laugh. If it was funny.

"So he came in and warmed his natty little backside on the hearth and asked if I'd given up drinking as well as living. I got the whisky out, and we had one of those pussyfooting conversations that Benny likes. The sort that sounds friendly on top and means something different underneath. He asked me why I'd sneaked out on him, and I told him the truth. I said I wanted to better myself and lead a quiet life. He didn't believe me. Being Benny, he thought I was running some sort of private racket and didn't want him to have a piece of it. He was feeling mean and he wasn't going to let me off the hook. He said that now I was here, I could make myself useful, and a place like this was just right for what he had in mind.

"We were drinking together as I haven't drunk since I left him —I've been a moderate man the last year, Reverend. A couple of glasses of wine of an evening. A pint in the pub. Anyway, I listened to him and kept filling his glass and mine, and nodding and smiling while Benny converted my house into a free hotel for wanted criminals and a private security vault for his hotter valuables.

"So I said to him, *I hope you haven't spread this visit all over the village, Benny, because if you have, you can forget the hide-out plan. If one person sprains an ankle here, everybody limps!*

"Never so much as mentioned you, my boy! said Benny. Just a friendly word in the local pub to make sure that they didn't scratch the Roller. Your estate agent had given me your address and drawn a map on the back of an envelope, and he mentioned the stones, which gave me an idea. So I told them I was just passing through, and being keen on stone circles, I wondered how near the road this one was and how could I get to it? I didn't have to mention your name. It turned up like a bad penny, old boy! But what a place to find! God, did that damned stone give me a scare when I shone a torch on it! Anyway, they very kindly advised me to come again by daylight, and I thanked them and left the Roller in the car-park.

"To give myself time, I pretended to go along with him. I said he was too smart for me—which he liked—and gave him the impression that his hunch wasn't entirely wrong. So he thought that he was on to a good thing and might even be on to a better one. Use a man's weakness against him, Reverend. That's one of my mottoes. Benny was always a vain man. So I flattered him. I got him to tell me how he'd found me—and he'd gone to some trouble!—and why he'd come tonight. He said it was on an impulse. He'd known my whereabouts for weeks, but there was no hurry. He'd been looking at a manor house near Reading that afternoon, with a view to buying it as a country seat—Benny collects houses like other people collect stamps!—and decided to drop in and surprise me. Then he showed me the brochure and asked my advice on one or two points. All mellow and self-satisfied, now that he thought he was getting his own way again."

He paused and then said conversationally, "Now I've bought myself a breathing space while I think things over, but the choice is simple. If I knuckle under, I'll never be free of him. If I don't, then he'll finish me one way or the other."

How could he think I was in any doubt?

I replied vehemently, "Harry! No matter what it costs, you must not give way to him even in the smallest measure."

He looked at me drily and answered, "My sentiments exactly, Reverend."

I have always been highly sensitive to atmosphere, and the house was so oppressive by this time that my collar felt uncomfortably tight. But my choice was also simple. I must do my duty by him, as a friend and as a priest. I knew it was useless to adopt a moral approach, so I attempted to be practical.

"You tell me this man runs a criminal organisation of a high order. Go to the police and tell them everything you know. You could in that way render an evil network and an evil man powerless."

He shook his head, saying, "Benny is very influential. It'd be me who got copped and did time. And he'd see it was a long time too! But we're agreed, at least, that Benny and his organisation should be—how did you put it?—rendered powerless. Yes, rendered powerless."

I nodded my head and clasped my hands, for I felt that this was a cruel thing to have happened to him and a cruel choice to make.

"Then I'll tell you what came into my mind the other evening. I'm speaking objectively, of course."

"Of course! Let us put it to debate!" I said, trying to lighten the atmosphere.

"Right. Now I thought, as Benny was sitting there, that I was being given a chance in a lifetime, because under the circumstances I could make it look like a different story. If you remember, Reverend, nobody knew he came here and we were alone. I thought, Supposing I killed him?"

Our glasses seemed to have emptied themselves, and I watched him refill them as if I were standing by the pair of us, looking on. I saw my hand take the glass and felt the swallows of brandy hot and strong down my throat while Harry peered into his darkness.

"Don't misunderstand me, Reverend," he said contemplatively, "I'm not a violent man by nature. But you see, if I got rid of Benny, I should kill two birds with one stone. Benny liked to play king, and he made sure that there was nobody else fit to wear the crown. His organisation is full of sidekicks. If he disappeared, it'd be like lifting a great big rock—a lot of nasty little things that depended on being hidden would come out."

My discomfort was both physical and emotional.

I heard myself say with difficulty, "There is good reason for the commandment that 'thou shalt not kill.' "

He laughed with genuine amusement. "Ah, that's the parson talking, not the thinker. The human race kills every day, Reverend. But let's not be sidetracked by arguments about vegetarianism or war. Let's stick to the case in point."

He was talking to himself as he had thought to himself.

"Now supposing I do kill him. How do I do it? Shoot him? Bash him on the head? No, I don't think so. Too much mess. Strangling is a different matter. Quiet and no blood. I'm a strong, fit man and Benny's only a whipper-snapper, so there'd be precious little struggle. It'd be over in no time. When I've finished, I bundle him inside a blanket and stick him in the stairs cupboard with the house-cleaning stuff.

"Now for the cover-up. I change my clothes for a pair of old trousers, a woollen sweater, and track shoes, and wear a dark mac over the lot. I pack my shaving kit, a railway timetable, and a bus timetable in my haversack. I put on a pair of woollen gloves, and I take his car keys and the brochure for his manor house. By this time it'll be well past midnight. I lock up the house and set out for the village. Everybody will have gone to bed long since. I find his Roller at the Green Man—looking like royalty at a jumble sale!—and I drive it as careful as can be, up to a car-park in Reading. By then it'll be about four o'clock in the morning. I doze on the back seat for a couple of hours, leave the brochure in the car, take the keys—to be disposed of later— find a men's lavatory, and shave there so that I look fresh.

"At Reading station I buy a return ticket so that I seem like a man on a walking holiday, and catch the first morning train to Exeter. From there I take a couple of buses and finally head for home over the fields on the other side of the village. So the first anybody sees of me that morning is coming over the stile, just a bit later than usual, to pick up my milk and post and newspaper.

They'll be too full of Benny and the Roller to notice me anyway, and I yarn with them for a bit, wondering what sort of a nut he must be! Then I walk back home."

I tried to remember whether anyone had mentioned Harry Bean coming into the village later than usual yesterday, but all the interest had of course been concentrated on the man in the Rolls-Royce. Besides, I reminded myself, this was only a supposition. A black and terrible supposition.

The room had lost its warmth and brightness. I sensed the weight of the house bearing down upon me, stone by stone. Sensed its presence as close and heavy as if it were standing behind me, listening, as mesmerized as I was.

He offered the cognac again, but this time I saw my hand, with a slight tremor, cover my glass.

He refilled his own steadily and said, "So Benny's dead and I've arranged a very creditable set of circumstances, where he disappears in Reading and they're going to have to find out why. Was he kidnapped in order to be held up to ransom? Did he do a moonlight flit because of dodgy dealings on the stock exchange? And so on. It'll be a while before they decide on a murder hunt. It's always possible that the long trail will lead to me in the end, but by then I'll have thought out another couple of moves ahead of them—that's why, most of the time, I beat you at chess, Reverend! No offence meant. All I have to do now is to dispose of the body, and there are plenty of ways and plenty of places for that. No problem at all."

He looked up at me in his old frank way and said, "Now, Reverend, I've fulfilled your conditions. I haven't given in to him and gone back to my old life. I've rid the world of an evil man, and his organisation will suffer a setback—which the police will make good use of. And, above all, I can go straight again, can't I? Apart from your moral scruples I'd say everybody was satisfied."

He was as pale as I was cold, and he kept his eyes fixed on mine. His hands were folded together, resting on the table in front of him.

Our intimacy had been established with a vengeance, and in

such a fashion that I felt more like a fellow conspirator than a friend. When I could speak, I heard my voice thick with shock and disbelief.

"Go straight? How can you do that? Your past is all about you. You live *on* it and *with* it and *in* it, under this unhallowed roof. You have broken both a moral and a social law. You will carry the burden of your guilt as long as you live."

He said coolly, lightly, watching me, "There'd be no guilt on my part and no repentance. I'm not the sort of man to do something without good reason, and once it's done, I wouldn't come crawling for absolution. No, that's the Christian in you talking, Reverend. But there are more things in heaven and earth than are dreamt of in your philosophy—or would you call that superstition?"

I had long since lost my objectivity, if indeed I had possessed it at all that evening, and I argued as passionately as if the crime had been committed in fact as well as in mind.

"I know what I call evil, and I acknowledge the attraction of evil," I replied, and my voice shook, not with fear but with earnestness. "And I speak of known facts, not superstitious fancies, when I say that no one who lived in this house ever prospered. No matter how finely you clothe it, Harry, it will still foment evil. In such a case as you have described, I would say that your past drew you here, Harry, and was used against you, and would be used against you until you were spent. There would be no going back."

In the long silence he watched me closely, flexing his fingers.

"All dark things draw darkness to them. Why should you stop with one murder, Harry? If you are prepared to kill to retain your freedom, then anyone who threatens you is at risk. And this much I say to you in all sincerity: you might burden me with a sin you were not prepared to repent or expiate, but you would not have my friendship. You would be on your own, in your house, with your secret. And to me that seems the darkest of all prospects."

He drew a deep breath through his nose, thinking. He took out his handkerchief and wiped a smudge from the glossy surface of the little table, then tucked it back into his pocket. And with the removal of the blemish he wiped out his mood and his expression. It was my old friend Harry Bean who looked back at me, smiling, and slapped both knees heartily.

"Well, I can't have that, Reverend!" he said. "I should have to play chess by myself then. Come! We've taken supposition far enough. Too far, perhaps. In which case I must ask you to excuse me. But we've never debated the question of life and death before."

Black chessmen faced white across the board. The game was still waiting to begin, but we had played some other game that evening and it had gone too near the bone for me. When I tried to answer him, I found my voice so hoarse that I used it as an excuse, saying something about a cold that became worse at night.

"Have a hot toddy!" he said, all concern.

I shook my head and rose so clumsily that I knocked the board awry and the pieces rolled all about.

Then Harry Bean laughed amiably, righting them, saying, "Surely, you didn't take me seriously, Reverend? Like I told you, I enjoy a good argument. I admit I'm in a tough spot at the moment, but I've been in tougher ones. Talking to you has helped me to put it into perspective. I'll sort it out somehow."

His laughter bruised me. I put on my coat and hat in silence.

He pursed his lips, judging my mood, and sighed before saying, "I'll see you out."

I lingered on his threshold a few moments, on pretence of turning up my collar against the cold. Outside, it was a strange moonlit world. In the distance, a dog barked and barked. I had always found it difficult to pass the stone image on such a night as this, and now I should need all of my strength. Still, the effort must be made, the first steps taken, the inward prayers said, if I was to find my way home again.

He did not shake my hand as usual, and I was glad of that as I walked slowly away from him. My feeling of claustrophobia closed in upon me as if I were muffled in a blanket. My feet were as heavy as if they were being dragged along the ground. At the top of the slope she stood there watching me, half-hidden in her grove of trees, and I stumbled and nearly fell before her. The ground beneath my fingers felt alive as I saved myself, sending a message through the cold, short grass which echoed my condition. Unable to rise, I crawled on my hands and knees from that unhallowed place.

It was long past the time of year when the women brought her a bunch of flowers and made a wish, so no one would come there. The weather was cold and crisp, but the ground not too hard, and I was a neat workman. In playing the sexton, I had cut the turf cleanly and rolled it back before I dug the grave, then relaid it afterwards so that it was hardly noticeable. Winter would be upon us soon, covering the traces, and by the time spring came, no one would tell the difference.

Above me, my accomplice, the Stone Mother, stood in watchful silence with her blood sacrifice at her feet, pointing a long black finger of shadow down the silver hill.

The Other Woman

David Williams

"Thanks, Gary. You can kiss me if you want," she said. And all I had to do was step closer. She did the rest—the first time, at least.

Well, she took me a bit by surprise—even me. It was only my second day in the job. We were in the master bedroom. I'd just driven her back from Guildford. She'd sat with me in the front of the Jag.

On the inward journey, her husband had been with us and they'd both been in the back. We'd dropped him at the station, then she'd gone shopping. She hadn't said much in the car, just watched me a lot, especially my hands. I'd taken the dress-shop bag upstairs as she'd ordered. It wasn't a heavy bag. I mean, she could have managed it herself, no strain. I'd wondered if she had anything else in mind. Then I'd thought, no such luck. I was wrong about that—if you'd call everything else that happened lucky.

"Not bad at all," she said, taking her mouth off mine, as if I was something she'd just eaten. Except the words had sounded more like a challenge than a compliment, that she'd expect me to do better next time. She hadn't let go of me either. "So when are you picking up Rick?"

"At five." Up to then, I'd called her "madam"; now it didn't seem right, not with the way she was groping me.

"Five? So what you waiting for?" She swivelled in my arms. "Undo my zip. Silly boy."

She was a fantastic lover.

"You really a public-school drop-out?" she asked later, when we were just lying on the open bed: it was mid-June and very hot. She was smoking a cigarette.

"I dropped out *after* school," I told her. The public-school bit always created interest—because I was a chauffeur.

Not that I'd ever been near a public school, but the idea went with the posh accent. I'd worked a lot on the accent since leaving my comprehensive in Manchester.

"My husband was impressed with your army service," she said.

I'd guessed that much. And my service record was pretty accurate; it needed to be, because it was easy to check—not like the other stuff. Like a few of the references, for instance. People never check on references. If they checked mine, they'd find most of the writers had gone abroad or died.

But the story of my five years in the Royal Electrical and Mechanical Engineers was kosher. The army taught me everything I'd ever need to know about car engines—enough to be an overworked fitter in a garage if I'd wanted. Only the part about refusing to go forward for a commission was invented.

"Why didn't you want to be an officer?"

I knew she'd be asking that. It works every time, especially with the birds. "I didn't want the responsibility," I said. "I like my freedom. It's why I stopped soldiering in the end too."

The last part was mostly true. Fact is, I've never really been a drop-out. I'm just someone who uses his skills to work for the biggest return over the shortest period and always with an eye to the main chance. But that's not the kind of thing you mention at a job interview.

Her husband was Colonel Rick Brota, mercenary extraordinary. He was retired, or else the call for hired assassins had dried up. That was what some locals in the village pub had said to me the night before. They didn't seem to like him.

I'd known already that Brota's speciality was masterminding military coups on islands where the government troops were underequipped or potentially disloyal, or both. He'd done a bit of the same in submergent Central Africa too. He hadn't always been successful. Except the word was, win or lose, he got paid in advance. The "freedom fighters" he'd worked for were always well bankrolled.

You could tell Brota had done well, from the shapes of his house and his wife. Mark you, he was getting on—over sixty, I reckoned, and writing his memoirs. With one eye and one arm lost along the way (he wore a black eye-patch but no artificial substitute for his right arm), he looked a bit of a crock, and he couldn't have been exactly a dashing military figure to begin with. He wasn't British for a start: Spanish or Portuguese, I'd guessed, up to then. He was small, gaunt, wizened, and asthmatic. He hardly ever spoke.

Of course, if he'd been in better nick, I wouldn't have risked taking instant liberties with his wife.

The house was stockbroker Tudor, air-conditioned throughout, with five acres of grounds and a chauffeur's flat over the garage. It stood by itself, backing on to woods, on the outskirts of a village southeast of Guildford, about thirty miles from London. I was engaged for chauffeuring and general maintenance. There was a lot of plant and machinery. Beryl, a middle-aged biddy from the village, came in early every day to clean the place and prepare the food. She left at noon and came back at six to cook and serve the dinner. There was a regular gardener on Mondays, Wednesdays, and Fridays.

It was now 1 P.M. on a Tuesday.

"You've got a very sexy body," she said, fingering bits of it.

"Not as sexy as yours." I was reciprocating in all senses.

I'd figured she was around thirty-five, three or four years older than me. Her first name was Connie, and she was an old-fashioned blonde bombshell. By which I mean she wasn't one of your flat-chested, underfed dollies held together with eye shadow. She was more the Marilyn Monroe type, if you remember her in her prime—or maybe just a bit past it.

Connie was tallish and well built all over, not fat, but plenty for a man to get hold of. She had big brown eyes, pouty lips, and tousled gold hair that she probably paid a lot to keep looking untamed. You wouldn't call her a raving beauty—her nose was a bit large—but she had real magnetism. She carried herself like an athlete or a dancer maybe—plenty of energy, with an urgent thrust in the upper-leg movements. And she had a grip like steel.

Socially Connie wasn't top-drawer. The heavy Mayfair accent had touches of Bermondsey that the charm school, or whatever, hadn't been able to iron out. It takes one to spot one.

"I've waited a long time for you to come along," she said later. We'd just finished another little orgy. She was sitting astride me at the time, massaging my chest. She seemed to like doing that.

"You mean you don't screw with all the new chauffeurs?"

Without any warning she slapped me hard across the face. Well, I suppose I'd asked for that. Then she slid off me and started weeping, back towards me.

"I'm sorry," I said. "I didn't mean that. I was only joking."

She didn't answer for a bit, just went on sobbing, fit to burst. Then she said, "You wouldn't joke if you'd been stuck here for five years with a has-been. It's no life for me. We've no friends. He never takes me anywhere. All he wants every night is to listen to Wagner recordings. And that's *really* all." She turned to look at me. "And I thought you were different. I could see you were interested. When we were in the car." She dabbed at those lovely eyes. "I'm not promiscuous, just desperate for affection. I have so much to give to anyone who'll really care for me!" She'd ended sounding bitter.

"I've said I'm sorry." I was, too, for nearly blowing everything. "So why do you stick it? A gorgeous woman like you?" I kissed her on the forehead.

"Because I used to think the swine couldn't last for ever. There was never any love between us. It was a marriage of convenience. We met through an up-market dating bureau. My previous husband ran out on me. Left me with a load of debt. Rick needed British nationality. He got that through the marriage."

By now she was recovering pretty fast.

"Why did he need the nationality?" I asked.

"In case they ever try to extradite him."

"Who?"

"Take your pick. There are half-a-dozen governments-in-exile who hate his guts. The ones he got deposed. If any of them ever got back in power, they'd want him strung up. After a show trial. It's an obsession with him. But he's sure the British would protect him."

"So what nationality was he?"

"Argentinian. Only they don't like him either. They'd have shopped him any time. To the first bidder. His first wife died years ago in Buenos Aires when he was away. The death certificate said heart attack. I've seen it. He thinks she was murdered."

"And he married you to get a British passport? So what did you get out of it?" I knew the answer, but it was polite to ask.

"His money. He's very rich." Well she was honest, at least. "As his wife, I get everything. That was the deal. Except he can go back on it. I can't."

"How can he go back on it?"

"By leaving me. Divorcing me. He's got what he wanted after all. They wouldn't cancel the nationality."

"But why should he divorce you?"

"Because he's found another woman."

"You're kidding?" He looked to me hardly capable of a good cough let alone . . .

"I wish I *was* kidding. I had him followed once. To where she lives in London. Afterwards I followed him myself. Twice last month. It's a block of service flats in Victoria. That's where he'll be today. Why he took the train. Otherwise you'd have been driving him. He's deadly secretive about her. Anyway, I've seen her. She's . . . she's older than me."

That last bit seemed to hurt the most.

"Why not tell him you know?"

"I wouldn't dare. In case he walks out on me."

"But if he did that, it's you who'd have the grounds for divorce."

She shook her head. At first I thought she wasn't going to explain, then she said, "He caught me with a man. It was two years ago. His name was Paul. He's an actor I'd known before.

When I was on the stage. We ran into each other again when he came to Guildford. To the theatre. It wasn't an affair, just a . . . a . . ."

"Renewing of an old acquaintance?" I helped her over the awkward bit.

"That's right. Rick didn't see it that way. He's insanely jealous. Possessive, even though he hardly ever wants me himself. I swore there was nothing lasting with Paul. But Rick made me promise in writing I'd never see him again. And I had to put that Paul and I'd been . . . been to bed together."

"Pity you did that."

"I'd no alternative. And now he's got that to hold over me."

She'd forgiven or forgotten my mistake by this time and was snuggling in my arms again.

"So what are you going to do?"

"Sometimes I think I'll kill myself. I would too. Or else kill Rick."

I didn't take the suicide bit seriously. It sounded too much as if she was playing for sympathy. And the idea of killing her husband was even less believable at the time.

It seemed to me she was a highly sexed, unsatisfied wife urgently in need of regular relief. So who better than Gary Powell to provide the necessary? And there were long-term possibilities on the cards as well. The job was going to be even more perfect than I'd hoped. The wages were well over the odds, with short basic hours and paid overtime to include all weekend work. Brota wasn't mean in that department. I had my own furnished flat, and the off-duty use of a four-year-old Honda 450-c.c. motorbike.

It was the sort of billet I'd been after for years. And while keeping madam happy would be no effort, I'd make sure I wasn't caught at it like Paul, her actor friend.

Meeting discreetly was easy—even on the days the gardener was around. There was no joy in the mornings because of the daily woman, but the afternoons were a cinch. Brota always slept a while then, if he was home. Later he'd go to his study and work on his memoirs. Connie would slip up to the flat, usually while he was sleeping. There was a door into the garage off the kitchen, and an inside stairs from the garage up to the flat, so no one ever saw her.

She still kept on about how miserable and trapped she was— and worried about Brota leaving her for this older bird. It was because I couldn't credit the other woman really existed that Connie finally got me to follow Brota and see for myself.

On the days I drove him to London—once or twice a week—I knew there was no chance he was seeing a woman. The routine was dead regular. In the morning I'd drop him at the British Library in Bloomsbury, pick him up and take him to his club in Pall Mall for lunch, then back to the library, and home from there at five. Sometimes it was other libraries or museums he worked in, but the routine was the same. I mean, this life story he was doing was serious work. Connie said he needed it to throw a whitewash over his gruesome past; she kept saying it.

Anyway, she was right about what he did in London when he went by train. On the day I mentioned, Connie drove him to Guildford station in her own car. She made the excuse that she'd sent me off early on an important errand on the Honda. That was nearly right too. I was parked opposite the house in Victoria when Brota arrived there in a taxi.

He didn't stay long—about half an hour. But when he left, the woman was with him. Connie was right. Her rival might have been a bit older, but that was the only minus. She was quite a looker—very dark, good figure, and the face of a madonna. They got into a taxi. I followed closely on the Honda. With the crash helmet on, my own mother wouldn't have spotted me. We finished up in Bedford Row. They went into a lawyer's office there and stayed two hours.

That convinced me.

Meantime, my affair with Connie was getting pretty torrid. I was crazy about her. She behaved in bed like no one else I'd ever known; don't get me wrong, but she had a real professional touch. The idea of losing her for any reason got to be unthinkable. You know how that can happen to a man with a very special woman?

"There's a way we could be together for always," she said to me one afternoon, as if she was reading my thoughts.

"How, lover?"

We were in my bed in the flat; it wasn't as big as hers in the house, but it was cosier.

"You know what he did for a living?" Connie asked, instead of answering my question.

"He was a mercenary."

"He murdered without cause or justification. For money."

"Other soldiers."

"Soldiers, civilians, women, and children." She shuddered. "He didn't discriminate. It's all in the filthy record. The one he's trying to cover up with this obscene biography. How can such a man live with himself?"

"I wonder that as well."

I remember her pulling her body closer to mine as she said, "If he committed suicide, no coroner would be surprised. With all that guilt weighing on him. I could say I'd seen it coming for years."

"He'd never do himself in?"

"But we could make it *look* as if he had! It'd be easy. And think of what we could do after? All that money? Over three million. Plus the house. Just for the two of us?" She thrust her open mouth over mine before I could answer.

In the next ten minutes Connie gave me a fantastic, unforgettable demonstration of what daily life could include, alone with her. It made all our other times together seem tame and lacklustre. It even made the money look simply like the icing on the cake.

It was then that I agreed to murder Colonel Brota.

Connie had the whole thing worked out. She had a dental appointment in London on the following Thursday afternoon. She would arrange with her husband that I should drive her there and back in the Jaguar, in case the treatment was painful. She knew he wouldn't want to go to town as well on Thursday, because he had fixed to go up the day before.

On the day, Connie and I would set off at one-fifteen. Close to London, I'd leave the car and switch to the Honda where I'd left it the night before. She would drive on, while I doubled back, stopping in the wood behind the house. I'd hide the bike there, and at two-thirty—the time Brota took his nap—slip up to my flat, using the garden gate to the wood. I'd change out of the clothes I was wearing, then go through the kitchen and hide in the hallway until Brota went to his study. He worked at a desk facing the window with his back to the door. He always left the door wide open.

Once he was busy, I'd creep up on him and shoot him with one of his own revolvers through the left side of his head. After I'd made it look like suicide, I'd change clothes again, pick up the Honda, and meet Connie at six o'clock where I'd left her. Later, we'd both swear we'd been together off and on all afternoon, that I'd waited outside in Sloane Street while she was at the dentist, then behind Harrods, where she'd have done some shopping.

We'd stop at the service station on the A3 near Esher. Connie would call the house from there. She'd speak to Beryl, the help, who'd be in the kitchen by then. Connie would explain we'd been held up by traffic and tell Beryl to warn Brota in case he got worried.

It was tough on Beryl, but she was a solid citizen, well able to stand shocks. We both agreed it was definitely better that we didn't find the body ourselves.

Connie had thought of everything. She even had a ready-made suicide note. It was a card written in Brota's own hand that said, *Forgive me. Rick.* It wasn't perfect, and it wasn't new, but it looked convincing enough. It was a note he'd done to go with some flowers he'd bought her after a quarrel three years before. She'd saved it; afterwards, I wondered if she'd been planning her husband's "suicide" all that time ago. I was to plant the note after I'd done the shooting.

The gun was no problem. There were four hand-guns in the

house—two service revolvers and two small automatics. One of the automatics was in the bedroom, but the others were kept in a locked drawer in the study; Connie had a duplicate key. It was she who decided I should use one of the revolvers, a single-action Webley 45. If Brota really had shot himself, she said, he'd have used a heavy gun: he thought of automatics as weapons for women. This was all right with me; I knew how to handle an army revolver—except I'd never shot anyone before.

Somehow Connie had me feeling that in wasting Brota, I was doing a public service. I suppose it was easier to think I was avenging all those women and children he'd liquidated.

When it came to it, the first part of the plan went like clockwork.

At three I was standing in the hall closet, watching Brota go into his study for what was to be the last time. Five minutes later I crept in behind him. He was bent over his work. There were open books all over the desk. He wrote everything in pencil, with his head close to the paper. He didn't wear glasses for his working left eye. The carpet was thick. I had on rubber sneakers. I know I made no sound getting up behind him. I moved slightly to his left as I started to raise the gun. I was holding it with both gloved hands; it was already cocked.

It was then that he sensed I was there. I'm certain it was nothing he heard; it was his training or something—uncanny. With no warning, without looking round, he rammed his chair backwards into me, throwing his body forwards and downwards, twisting around clockwise, to the right, scattering books and papers like confetti.

The next moment he was crouched in the knee-hole of the desk; then he was starting at me like a spring uncoiling—and there was a bloody great flick knife gleaming in his only hand. The chair had caught me in the groin, off-balance and off-guard. I'd fallen back, nearly fallen over, but I didn't panic. It stayed in my mind that I had the best weapon, that I had to shoot him, that I had to shoot him close-to, and that nothing else would fit for a self-inflicted wound.

Although I was scared, I let him come at me. He'd used the

chair again, jumping on to it, levering off the seat as if a cat, so he ended aiming himself downwards at me, like he was flying. He didn't shout or speak, just made sharp groaning breaths that I'll never forget.

For a split second I didn't move; then I ducked and feinted to the left. As he passed me, I brought up the revolver again double-handed and squeezed the trigger. The gun went off with a roar. I thought the muzzle was pretty close to his head.

Brota hit the floor with the far side of his skull exploded by the exit wound. There was blood splattered all over him—none of it mine, though. It had been a good try for an older guy, but he hadn't touched me. I'd managed to stay out of knife range. He'd been leading with his left; it was all he had to lead with, poor sod. I'd dodged the other way.

I'd dodged to my left.

It only came home to me the second time. Even then I had to look again before it sunk in.

His skull was a mess all right, because of the heavy calibre of the weapon—except the clean bullet entry hole was on the right side of the head. I'd missed out on one thing when he'd turned on me.

I suppose I'd been so obsessed about getting the gun close and so thrown at his resisting at all, I'd forgotten I had to shoot him on the left side. Not that I could have done much else anyway. If I'd feinted the other way, he'd probably have got me with his knife.

As I moved the chair behind the body, I was telling myself that a man with only a left arm just might decide to shoot himself through the right temple.

I kept telling myself that.

Otherwise things weren't a lot different from the way we'd planned.

I didn't try putting him into the chair. It would have to look as if pushed it back, stood up and turned around before he'd shot himself. I left him exactly where he'd fallen, being careful not to step where there was any sign of blood. There was some blood on the sleeves of my shirt, but I'd allowed for that.

I took the flick knife from Brota's hand and put the gun in its place. I wiped the knife, closed it, and put it on the desk, then buried it under books I picked up off the floor. It was where it must have been at the start.

I left the suicide note on the desk blotter—lying on the centre of a clean sheet of paper.

Going back to the flat, I took off the shirt and jeans and made a bundle of them. I put on my chauffeuring clothes again, under my bike gear, all except my suit jacket, which was in the car.

I left the property the same way I'd come, without being seen by anyone: I was sure of it. Once on the road, I was just another motorcyclist buried under tin-lid and ton-up gear. I stuffed the clothes bundle into a half-full builder's skip outside a clearance job.

I was back at the meeting place ahead of Connie. We'd fixed it that way so she wouldn't be seen sitting in a big parked car, looking conspicuous on the edge of Wimbledon. It was safe enough to leave the bike there.

She was over the moon that I'd done the job. She wasn't so pleased when I told her exactly where I'd shot him, not any more than I was. We'd both known the importance. After a bit, she agreed the police would accept that Brota had chosen to shoot himself in a cack-handed way—because what other explanation was there?

Connie made the phone call at the service station.

"OK?" I asked when she got back in the car.

"It should be, in a minute," she said. "When Beryl gets to the study."

"If she rings the police straight away, they ought to be there in ten minutes." I was timing it so we'd be home in half an hour.

Connie didn't say anything for a bit.

"You all right?" I asked later. She was frowning.

"Look, in case anything goes wrong, that's for both of us or just one of us, let's make a pact."

"About what?"

"The money. Rick's money." She paused. "Half each."

"But we'll be spending it together," I was trying to be cheer-

ful, but I knew what was in her mind and why. It was I who'd
cocked things up.

"I mean *if* things go wrong, if one of us has to skip, or anything. We should be prepared."

"And by 'anything,' you mean me ending up in the nick?" I
said, and I wasn't joking.

"That could happen to both of us. But if it does, or just to one
of us, when it's over, still half each?"

"That's fair." What she meant was, if I got rumbled and she
didn't, my half would be waiting for me when I'd done time.
"But I still don't see—"

"And neither of us admits anything," I remember her interrupting, her voice very firm. "Whatever happens, we agree to
stick to the story?"

"Sure."

I think my optimism started draining from then.

When we got to the house there were two police cars, two ordinary cars, and an ambulance in the drive. Beryl had done her bit.

Connie acted as if she'd been born to the part. Surprise, shock,
horror, hysterics, all came in the right order. In no time, she was
being helped to her bedroom, weighed down with inconsolable
grief. It was left to me to explain where we'd been, except Beryl
had done a good advance job over that too. I was just as bowled
over as the loving wife, but in a manly, loyal way.

"Yes, the colonel had been depressed. For the last three days,"
I answered the direct question. It seemed to satisfy them at the
time. "I couldn't say whether he had frequent fits of depression.
I've only been employed here five weeks." Then they wanted to
know how I'd got the job, where I'd worked before, and before
that. They seemed almost as impressed with the army bit as
Brota had been. I didn't bother with the up-market trimmings,
though.

The questions appeared pretty routine, but they went on a bit:
"Yes, I knew the colonel had been a mercenary," and, "No,
there hadn't been any visitors expected that afternoon," and

again, "No, I hadn't seen any strangers hanging about the place."

There were two of them doing the asking, both CID—a Detective Inspector Stewart and a Detective Sergeant Montgomery.

"It's pretty certainly suicide, Mr. Powell," the inspector said, like he was taking me into his confidence. "But we have to check all possibilities, you understand?"

"Of course," I said, relaxing a bit.

"Where's the motorbike, Mr. Powell?" Montgomery asked suddenly.

I'd been ready for that one. I said I'd taken it to Wimbledon the night before, to a special dealer, because of a dodgy clutch I couldn't fix myself. But the dealer had been closed. So I'd left the bike and thumbed a lift back, not wanting to risk any more damage to the gearbox.

"You didn't use it this afternoon?" That was the sergeant again.

"No. How could I? I was driving Mrs. Brota."

"Of course," Stewart chipped in. He nodded and smiled before he changed the subject. "The colonel and his wife, what sort of terms were they on?" he asked. "Good terms, would you say?"

"Very good terms. Very loving. So far as I could see. But like I said, I haven't been here that long." I didn't want to overdo it.

And that was nearly it. I had to give them a timetable of where we'd been in the afternoon, and they wanted to know exactly where the Honda was, as well as its licence number. More routine, the inspector said. They didn't mention exactly how Brota had shot himself. There was nothing said either about how the shot was fired or about his only having one arm—the wrong one for aiming a gun at the right temple.

There were police about the place till nearly midnight. They left then. The body had been taken away earlier. It looked as if it was all over, except they locked and sealed the study—door and windows. Said it would have to stay that way till after the inquest; it was understandable, I thought.

Connie was left to herself, but not totally alone. The local doctor came and gave her a sedative. He said she should have someone sleeping in the house for the night. Beryl volunteered, so we had no celebration that night—not that we'd have risked it in any case.

Stewart and Montgomery came back next morning at eight-thirty. I was hosing the Jag when they arrived. They waved to me but didn't speak. It was a detective constable who came later who asked to see my crash helmet and the rest of my bike gear. His car was pulling a trailer; the Honda was on it.

The two senior coppers were in the house for over two hours. When Beryl brought me a cup of coffee at ten-thirty—she always did that—she said they'd been alone with Connie since before nine.

When they came round to the garage I was doing a job on the work-bench. They asked to talk to me in the flat upstairs. They wanted to know again if I'd used the bike the previous afternoon. I answered the same as before. Then they said someone had been seen getting out of a blue Jaguar in Wimbledon, dressed in identical bike-gear to mine, at one fifty-eight, and then ridden off on a bike like mine. I said it couldn't have been me. Montgomery said Mrs. Brota had just had to admit it was me. That I'd left her around two and met her again later.

Apart from sweating all over, wanting to be sick, and wishing the world would stop, I had to think like lightning. If Connie had said that much, she'd have to have been desperate.

I made the decision: "OK. It's a fair cop," I said, looking a bit ashamed. "The colonel never gave me time off in the day. Mrs. Brota's more understanding. When I drive her to London, she sometimes drops me off for the afternoon. There's a girl in Croydon I've been seeing if I've got the bike handy. She works nights. It's what happened yesterday. Except I found the girl's gone away."

"Why didn't you tell us this before, Mr. Powell?" Stewart asked.

"Because when we got back, with the suicide and everything,

I thought I'd best stick to what we'd have told the colonel. That's if he'd asked."

" 'We' being you and Mrs. Brota?"

"I didn't want to let her down, like."

Montgomery stood up after his boss gave him the nod. "Mr. Powell," he said, "I have to tell you we have reason to believe that after you left Mrs. Brota, you came back here, concealed the motorbike in the wood, shot Colonel Brota dead, and later rode back to Wimbledon."

"That's a lie," I said. "A diabolic lie."

But I was convicted of murder three months later.

I never talked to Connie again, but I stuck to our agreement. I never admitted anything—still haven't. I always reckoned it was police harassment that got her saying I'd left the car.

The rest of the evidence was all circumstantial. The shot had been made too far from the right temple for Brota to have fired it himself with his left hand. There were fine traces of his blood on the knife, even though it had been wiped, closed, and deliberately hidden under papers on the desk. The house had been locked tight, as always, because of the cooling system, with no signs of a break-in. I was the only one with a key besides Beryl, who'd been at a Mother's Union meeting all afternoon. Two local women had seen a motorbike in the wood when they'd walked a dog there at three. They'd thought it was my bike, and it was gone when they came back later. The ink on the "suicide note" showed it was more than two years old.

None of these things amounted to that much on its own. But when you put them all together they were enough for a jury— and an appeal court later.

My story is still that I'm the victim of a miscarriage of justice. That way, there's always hope that if you keep on, some do-gooder will take up the case, shake somebody's testimony, and get you pardoned; it happens all the time, if you wait for the dust to settle and memories to dim. You have to stick to your testimony, though.

Connie never got implicated. There was a time at the start

when I thought she would be for sure. That was when they tried to get me to involve her, saying that if I admitted she put me up to the murder, I'd get a lighter sentence. They said the same to my lawyer. But I couldn't see any real benefit in it, even if I'd been ready to shop her, which I wasn't. Whichever way you looked at it, I'd have had to admit I'd committed a crime in the first place. There was no point in both of us serving time if one could stay in the clear, looking after the money.

They suspected her all right, but no jury would have convicted Connie in her widowhood. The director of public prosecutions must have seen that, even if the police didn't. In the end, it was his decision not to charge her, or so my lawyer said. They figured a jury would say I hadn't been around long enough to have had anything going with the colonel's wife, on top of which her grief had everyone convinced. In court it bloody near convinced me. She came there as a prosecution witness against me; that must have been part of the deal with the DPP. Of course, she didn't shop me altogether—only said I'd been off alone for the afternoon. Well, she'd been made to admit that already; I've never found out how. Anyway, I didn't blame her. The foul-up was still down to me.

I think they lost interest in Connie when some*thing*, or some-*one*, put them on to a motive for the murder that didn't involve her and made it seem I'd used her without her knowing. At the end, they'd definitely persuaded themselves I'd been put up to the job as a contract killing, by one of Brota's old enemies, and everyone knew there were plenty of those to chose from. It was why they didn't expect me to grass. My being an ex-soldier fitted too.

I thought even if I had to do eight years of the "life" sentence before parole, I still had something to look forward to. I didn't include Connie as part of the something—that was being realistic, especially after her actor friend Paul got permission to see me following the appeal hearing. He was a good-looking bloke, officer class from birth, I could see that. Connie had sent him to tip me the wink that my share would be waiting as promised. At the same time, he made it pretty clear I wasn't to expect a share of Connie as well.

So imagine the surprise when I saw this law report in the paper. It said Mrs. Eva Brota, second wife of Colonel Rick Brota, had been to court to claim the whole of her husband's estate. Fair enough I thought at first, wondering why she'd had to go to court and why they'd got her first name wrong. But it went on to say it was Connie who'd *lost* the case. It was then I noticed there were pictures of two women. I recognised the dark one as well, from the time I followed her and Brota from Victoria to the lawyers.

This Eva had been his second wife all right, with an Argentine wedding licence to prove it. He'd married her, then later deserted her and two children, years ago. That was in some South American outback village, where he'd been hiding while the heat was on. She'd been no more than a peasant then—so she'd improved herself since. But she'd still thought he was dead until a few months before, the same as he must have hoped she was; to my knowledge he'd never mentioned her to Connie.

When Eva found out her husband was alive and loaded and living in England, she'd come over demanding maintenance. The report said they'd had "several meetings alone and with their lawyers to work out a secret settlement." The circumstances for Brota, it said, had been "very delicate."

Well, dying had settled every kind of delicate circumstance for him, but not for her; it also produced an outsize delicate circumstance for Connie.

Brota had been trying to keep Eva's existence quiet to protect his British nationality—because he'd known she was putting that on the line. Eva could prove his marriage to Connie was bigamous, and like all bigamous marriages, the paper said, this one was null and void, "along with all benefits stemming to either party." But even though one of those null-and-void benefits was Brota's new nationality, you wouldn't have guessed that could hurt anyone now. It did though. A bigamous wife has no rights.

The report said the judge expressed his sympathy to Connie. But Eva got all the money.

About the Editor

The Winter's Crimes series was created in 1968 by George, Lord Hardinge of Penhurst. Hilary Hale (then Hilary Watson) edited the eighth volume, and thereafter, she and George edited alternate years until his retirement in 1986. Hilary Hale, now the sole editor, is Editorial Director for crime fiction at Macmillan London Ltd.